DRONE CHASE

DRONE
CHASE

PAM WITHERS

DUNDURN
TORONTO

Publisher: Scott Fraser | Acquiring editor: Kathryn Lane | Editor: Susan Fitzgerald
Cover designer: Laura Boyle
Cover image: drone: istock.com/fitie; mountain landscape: istock.com/askinkamberoglu
Printer: Marquis Book Printing Inc.

Library and Archives Canada Cataloguing in Publication

Title: Drone chase / Pam Withers.
Names: Withers, Pam, author.
Identifiers: Canadiana (print) 20200214527 | Canadiana (ebook) 20200214543 | ISBN 9781459747432 (softcover) | ISBN 9781459747449 (PDF) | ISBN 9781459747456 (EPUB)
Subjects: LCGFT: Novels.
Classification: LCC PS8595.I8453 D76 2020 | DDC jC813/.6—dc23

We acknowledge the support of the Canada Council for the Arts and the Ontario Arts Council for our publishing program. We also acknowledge the financial support of the Government of Ontario, through the Ontario Book Publishing Tax Credit and Ontario Creates, and the Government of Canada.

Printed and bound in Canada.

VISIT US AT

 dundurn.com | @dundurnpress | dundurnpress | dundurnpress

Dundurn
3 Church Street, Suite 500
Toronto, Ontario, Canada
M5E 1M2

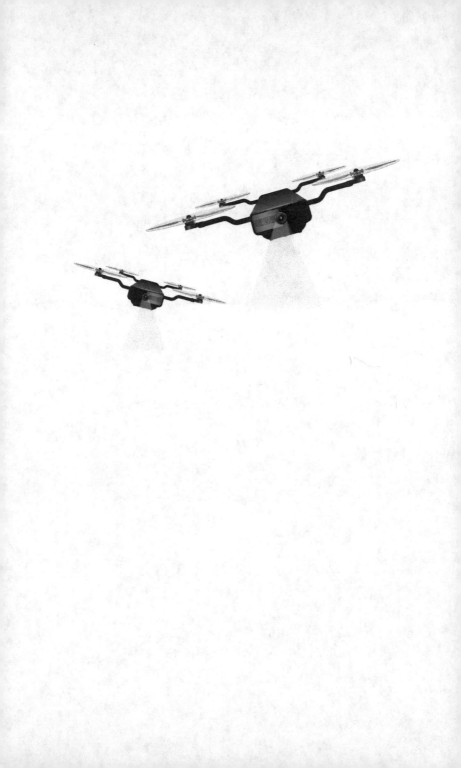

CHAPTER ONE

HUDDLED IN A down parka, with my hands held to the camp-fire, I glance down the slope to make sure my parents are still on their walk. Affirmative: Their bickering voices — they haven't stopped fighting since we moved here — are disturbing the afternoon peace of the mountainside. Next, I peer at the little red tent a few feet away from me. My sleeping granddad's unlaced hiking boots are sticking out from under the flap. In fact, the whole tent is shuddering with his snoring like a half-inflated balloon.

Zzz-zzz. The sound lifts my mood. It's a good thing whiskered old mountain men need afternoon snoozes. Here at last, an opportunity to escape this boring, chilly campsite in the Canadian boonies.

It's not the first time this city boy has been hauled unwillingly here, into a desolate land of granite peaks, waterfalls, dodgy wildlife, and monster trees, but it's definitely not somewhere I feel at home. For one thing, dark woods scare me, and this place has endless trees. I hate trees. They have a bad habit of eating my drones.

Camping in general, in my private opinion, sucks. Who willingly goes for a hike in the sticks in May? Give me Central Park muggers any day over perilous predators hiding behind giant, moss-draped trees. I'm a New York City guy through and through.

I reach into the beefy backpack Granddad has saddled me with — "It'll toughen you up," he said — and touch the cellphone-sized drone the old man and my parents don't know I've smuggled along. It's a perfect antidote to the eerie woods.

"Remote-control toys are for kids," Granddad ruled in his Irish brogue last month when my parents and I arrived. "They're for city-park shenanigans. Got to get you in shape, teach you about woodsmanship, pry you out of that workshop o' yours. Real life is the mountains, kid, and I'm going to teach you and yer city mom backcountry survival and appreciation for nature."

Like that's going to happen. As far as I can tell, Granddad has hated my "city mom" ever since she "stole away" his son to the other side of the continent. Given her high heels, makeup, New York personality, and lack of enthusiasm for the outdoors, in his mind she's beneath his contempt. Which caused friction on our vacations here as far back as I can remember. But now that we've actually moved here, it's way worse.

Sitting close to where we've strung up the food bag on a rope between two trees — "to make it fierce-hard for bears to reach it, grandson" — I pull out my fifteen-hundred-dollar store-bought drone kit: bird, batteries, and remote. The drone is four wavy rings joined by a centre that resembles a small bug. I call him Bug. The 250-millimetre, one-pound device can fly for about twenty minutes before he conks out. Then, clever robot that he is, he automatically returns to me. Another thing: He folds so neatly I can slip him into my jeans pocket. As in, I can hide him from Granddad's sharp eyes.

We're with Granddad because Dad tore us away from New York City. Granddad, an expert hunter and outdoorsman I admire but will never be like (as he reminds me regularly), lives in Bella Coola, in northern British Columbia. Bella Coola (population 150) is located in a mountain valley on a saltwater inlet maybe sixty miles — or I guess I should say a hundred kilometres, since I'm in Canada — east of the Pacific Ocean, in the heart of the Great Bear Rainforest. Dad says we had to move here because Granddad's health is "failing." Failing? To me, the dude is stronger and more stubborn than a nine-hundred-pound grizzly — and grizzlies actually live in the forests around here. Granddad is a headstrong taxidermist who stuffs and mounts dead furry animals for clients. So disgusting.

According to Dad, Granddad's terminal cancer means he doesn't have many months to live. It's true he's not as tough as he used to be, but there's still plenty of griz left in him. And while he afternoon-hibernates, I'm outta here. Yes, I'm supposed to stick close to camp, and yes, the woods are full of dangerous stuff that scares me to death. But the trees aren't dense and dark right around camp, and it's a chance to launch a drone, which is what I'm all about.

I grab the bear-spray can and stuff it into my designer moto jeans pocket. Though I definitely hope I won't meet a nasty bruin, I pretend I'd have the nerve to fire the peppery stuff into one's face if I had to. Slapping away early-spring flies, I follow a path to a small clearing. *Concentrate on the drone, not where the forest gets darker just up the slope. And don't freak out if you see a bear. That ended badly last time.*

I unfold the drone's arms and click in all four propellers, or props. Next, I give the 4K-sensor mini-camera a quick wipe-down, attach it to the body, and set the drone on the dewy grass of the clearing. After charging up my radio-sized remote controller for takeoff, I take a big step back and a deep breath and throw the throttle stick up. Yes! My slick graphite baby rises on cue and hovers in front of me with a happy hum.

A surge of excitement ripples through my body, like it does no matter how many times I do this. Flying allows me to de-stress, to take a break from missing my New York City friends and worrying about Mom and Dad's recent arguing or Granddad's cancer. When I'm flying my drones, even ominous woods turn into my happy place for awhile.

When the machine reaches four hundred feet (picture a forty-storey building), I admire Bug's bird's-eye view from the mini-tablet, slid onto my remote controller. Then, like the ace pilots I admire, I hit the throttle of the remote, tilting and thrusting till even I can appreciate Bug's camera view of the crazy-tall trees, seriously blue sky, and icy glaciers that look like someone has spilled green Slurpees all over the mountaintops. I spot hairy mountain goats hanging out on a ridge and a real live eagle swooping high above them.

Imagining myself as a miniature pilot in my drone, I bank left, barrel-rolling for the crowds below, dogfighting with the drones of my New York City friends, Arlo and Koa. What I wouldn't give to be back there with them.

Whoa! A nasty gust of wind catches my little guy. I do my best to keep him steady. But my remote controller starts beeping like crazy, warning me that Bug is losing connection to the controller because of wireless interference. Next thing I know, he is spinning out of control toward a tree. My fingers yank on the joystick, but I can't get whatever's loose to reconnect.

I hit the return-to-home button in a desperate attempt to save Bug. He doesn't respond — Nooo! — just clips a branch and free-falls toward the ground. At least I see where he's landed. Stumbling through the brush, I head that way, trying not to trip over stupid roots or slip on damp moss.

Phew! He is not so far away, just into the woods, on a small hillock of dirt half blocking a hole in the base of a giant cedar. In fact, my baby has parked himself partway into the entrance, like he's shivering and wants a garage. As I sprint toward my flying machine, I see no cracks or breaks. I sigh in relief. We just might've gotten lucky.

Except — my stomach tightens as I draw closer — for the smoke coming out of Bug's far side. Wait, no. Not out of the drone. Out of the garage. And not smoke but —

No way. Breath! Someone or something is inside the tree breathing in the chill air. Something with a wet, black nose. Behind the nose, a massive bear's head pushes out of the gap and gives an unholy growl, deep and menacing, like a Rottweiler crossed with a sasquatch.

My eardrums vibrate like a subway's running through my head, and terror electrifies every nerve. But even through the panic, I reach forward to scoop up my drone. I'm that kind of dad. Then I stagger back, tucking him into the back pocket of my jeans.

"Most o' the bears around here are still asleep," Granddad told my parents and me before this weekend's camping trip. "To be sure, if we do run into one, climb a tree quick smart if it's a grizzly. If it's a black bear, drop face first to the ground, wrap yer arms around yer head and neck, and play dead. Never, ever run."

Every cell in my body screams, *Run*. But channelling all the self-discipline I can, I force myself to freeze as the bear emerges. Grizzly or black bear?

I recall Granddad's lectures. "Grizzlies have up-turned noses, small ears, shoulder humps, and long, straight claws."

I have no idea which brand this girl is, but she's one big customer. Seven feet tall, hairy as Chewbacca, and smelly as rancid oil. No more than fifty feet away, she's clacking her teeth, flaring her nostrils, and making a sound like *whoosh*. Worse, two cubs the size of full-grown St. Bernards bound out of the tree like fluffy puppies, tumbling around Mama's very large ass.

While frantically weighing my options, I stand tall, meet the bear's eyes, and attempt to project calm instead of terror. Being the kid of two veterinarians, I know a thing or two about animals. It's super important they don't sense panic or fear. In my parents' clinic, I've always had a skill for calming dogs. My parents call me the animal whisperer.

So, get a g-g-grip, Ray. Ref-f-frame the situation. Use h-h-humour. After all, I'm not a morning person either, and I've disturbed this brute and her babies from their long winter nap.

A side glance reveals a tall evergreen with low, sturdy branches that even a gymnastically challenged slackwad might be able to scramble up. With one hand on my bear-spray can, I take a step toward it, super slow-mo.

"Never get between a sow and her cubs," Granddad always warns. "Just talk to the beast respectful-like as you back away."

"Sorry, Blondie," I say in as even a tone as I can manage. Blond equals grizzly, my half-paralyzed brain informs me. "My little drone didn't mean to wake you up. He was just crash-landing." I chance another step toward the tree. "He wasn't going to hurt one of your little ones."

The bear stomps her front feet, flattens her ears, gives me a spine-chilling glare, and lowers her head straight-on. I know in my gut she's going to charge. As my spongy knees miraculously support the final two steps to the tree, I leap onto the first branch and struggle to do my first pull-up since last year's sophomore gym class, where I was pretty useless. Then I scramble upwards, fuelled by rocket-booster-grade adrenalin.

With a roar that sets pine needles quivering, Mama Bear lunges and in one bound reaches the tree. She raises her hairy shoulders high and rests her massive paws against the trunk just feet below my flailing silver running shoes (new, and purchased at great expense from Hell's Kitchen Flea Market in Manhattan).

My heartbeat ups by a factor of three, my teeth form a death clench, and sweat streams out of my pits. Her next bellow is loud enough to wake up the valley and raise all three hairs on my chest.

When she quiets for a second, I try to speak to her calmly, like I do to upset dogs in our clinic. "I'm planning to stay up here till you go back to sleep or a rescue helicopter shows, okay?" Talking to animals: yeah, it's a thing in veterinary clinics.

Then I screech, "Mom! Dad! Granddad! A bear!" Maybe I shouldn't have wandered away from our campsite after all?

The cubs peek out at me from behind their mother's tank-sized body. To keep my panic in check, I shift my eyes to one of them, a little guy trembling like a toddler hidden in its mother's skirts. Its whimper tugs at my heart. It's like a carnival-prize giant teddy bear, with a cute brown nose and very pink mouth, which opens wide to emit a wail like a baby's.

It might be five minutes. It feels like an hour. I clutch the tree's upper branches with moist hands and watch the mother bear as she watches me. I half wish I hadn't shouted. The last thing I need is my unarmed parents or weakened granddad scrambling up the slope right now.

I catch movement from the corner of my eye and hear three blasts.

I cry out as the sow drops heavily to the ground, bleeding from the front of her steep forehead. She lands on the cub who was wailing, trapping it beneath her giant bulk. I turn my shuddering body toward my granddad, who is standing there holding a rifle, looking proud.

My chin trembles and my shoulders quake as I look from my murderous granddad to the second panicked cub as it scampers away, then halts as if torn over what to do. The one beneath its mother is bellowing in pain. A cold heaviness creeps into my chest.

CHAPTER TWO

"BEGORRAH! I DID IT!" Granddad shouts with a grin, adjusting his stiff-brimmed Donegal tweed wool cap just as I spot my wide-eyed parents staggering up the rise behind, my mother tripping, my father breathing heavily. "When they charge," Granddad continues excitedly, "it's the brain or spine you have to hit. Even with five-shot capacity, my forty-five-seventy high-calibre rifle needed total accuracy on the first round. Are you okay, Ray? Bejesus, you've had a scare, and nearly sent my ticker over the brink, too." He frowns. "Aha, I see your drone in your pocket. That explains why you wandered, eh?"

Unable to speak, unwilling to drop out of my tree, I watch the second cub inch back to its mother's still form and push its soft nose into her. Its trapped sibling produces another pathetic cry, making the free one swivel its head from it to me.

I gaze at my gloating granddad. "You killed the mother," I finally choke out.

"I did!" Granddad smiles and turns to my dad.

"Shouldn't we rescue the cub under her body?" my mother asks, standing tall and slim behind my dad. She's wearing tight jeans and a red cashmere sweater, with matching bracelets and earrings.

"Whatever," says Granddad.

Dad speaks up. "I'll fetch your capture pole and cage from the back of the Jeep."

Capture pole? What's that? And doesn't anyone care about soothing my nerves just now?

"No need to capture the yearling," Granddad objects. "Just free it from under the sow and let nature take its course."

"No way," Mom pleads with Dad. "It might be hurt."

"Stay out of it. You don't know what yer talking about," Granddad says to her in a harsh tone, making me wince and her flush. She looks squint-eyed at Dad, her red suede boots planted firmly on the ground, her lipsticked lips pressed together.

"We'll just check it for injuries first," Dad says, and hoofs it down the slope. Granddad and Mom face each other in silence, arms crossed. Minutes later, Dad returns with a large dog cage and a four-foot-long aluminum pole featuring a circle of plastic dangling from one end — a circle like a noose. He's also carrying a minimal veterinary first-aid kit. He pulls out a muzzle and a syringe for, I'm guessing, giving the cub a sedative.

I watch, sickened, as Mom puts the muzzle on the cub. Dad and Granddad roll the sow over like she's a heavy carpet roll, like just minutes ago she wasn't a living, breathing animal defending her babies.

The men hold down the cub, having thrown a coat over its flailing paws. Finally, before the crushed thing can move, my father lowers the noose around its neck and uses a device on the handle to pull it tight. The small bear screeches as it paws its throat, half-suffocated. My fingers curl into my palms. The other sibling gallops off.

Loosening the snare a little, Mom and Dad bend over and examine their patient.

"Broken paw," Mom diagnoses, and administers an intramuscular injection of painkiller into the yearling's hind end. Then they push the animal into the dog cage as casually as if it's a long-time pet. In fact, it probably weighs more than a hundred pounds.

It bawls like crazy. I can't help frowning. "Why do you have a noose pole and cage in your Jeep?"

Granddad shrugs. "Never know what you might need up here in the mountains, grandson. Though, personally, I'd have let this thing fend for itself." He shoots a disapproving look at my mom.

"A newly orphaned cub with a broken paw fend for itself in the wild?" my mother challenges.

"Yearling, not cub," Granddad informs her, like he's speaking to a child. He pulls his phone from his pocket. "I'll call Evan Anderson, the conservation officer, to come deal with the sow's carcass. Maybe he'll give me the head to mount."

"And the one that ran away?" I dare to ask.

"Half-grown and old enough to survive on its own," Granddad says. I'm not convinced.

"Thank goodness Dad got there in time and was armed. So lucky you weren't hurt," my father says when we reach the Jeep. I climb mutely into the front passenger seat. The caged yearling bangs around in the back. It smells ripe. Putrid. But I don't care. A part of me wants to climb into the back and comfort it.

"Did you really have to kill the mother?" I ask Granddad, still shaken.

I mean, I've lived most of my life in New York City, where there are random homicides every hour. But I've never seen a murder up close and personal.

"Saints preserve us! It was you or it," Granddad says as he hoists himself into the driver's seat.

"For sure," says Dad.

I turn around in time to see Mom shake her head before she climbs into the back seat, well away from Dad.

Granddad shoves the key into the ignition. "You, boy, learned up a good lesson after going arseways. Next time use the bear spray."

Like Mom, I can never do anything right when it comes to Granddad. But reminding myself that he's ill, I don't respond to his biting words.

"It was especially dangerous being distracted by flying your drone," Dad weighs in, clutching my confiscated Bug.

"Lucky? Lesson? He was almost killed!" Mom bursts out as she presses herself against the passenger door. I turn back to stare out the front windshield. "I told you this place was dangerous. It was a crazy idea bringing us up here. We almost just lost our son, Sean. Does that mean anything to you?"

"Almost lost yer son? Don't be stupid, woman," Granddad says.

"It was Ray or the bear," Dad says, trying to soothe her as Granddad starts up the Jeep and pulls away from our campsite. "And Ray actually handled it pretty well, considering. Anyway, bear encounters are part of life here. But, hmm, does that thing ever stink."

"It's scared." I defend it, breathing through my mouth.

"Well, I hate it here," Mom says. "Now I've said it! Please, Sean, I want to move back to Manhattan. And so does Ray."

I open my mouth to protest, but stay silent when my granddad gives me a curt headshake. The old man then careens around a curve on this poor excuse for a logging road.

It is not 100 percent true I want to move back to New York City after only a month in Bella Coola, the three-block town we can see in the long, green valley below us as the Jeep moves along the mountainside road. Several tiny towns and many green farms line the river that flows between heavily forested, snow-capped mountains. I shade my eyes to try to spot the farm where, I'm told, a moose guards the cows from mountain lions. I have to admit the valley is picturesque, even if it is entirely capable of giving a New Yorker a serious case of boredom and culture shock. I'm still angry Dad forced the move on us. I've yelled at him a lot for it. I miss my city friends and school so much it hurts. I still text or talk with my friends every few nights. Plus, Mom and Dad never fought back there, only here, thanks to the Granddad factor. But despite all that, I'm trying not to be as stubborn and closed-minded as Mom. I'm afraid if I agree with her, my parents' arguing will get worse. And, sometimes, I actually enjoy hanging out with Granddad.

"New York's not home anymore, Leah. You agreed to move but you haven't even given it a chance. Ray's trying. He's at least trying. And there's my father to consider."

Do my parents even know Granddad and I are sitting right in front of them? Do they care how *I* feel about Mom's chilling pronouncement or my near-death experience in the stupid woods? Am I invisible to them these days? Doesn't anyone feel bad about the mother bear, the runaway cub, or the injured orphan? And, just for once, can't they stop fighting about the move?

"Ray survived," Granddad says offhandedly. "And he'll pull up his socks here eventually." He glances at me. "Yer just like yer dad," he says, "a bit of a jackass. But I reckon he knew more than you before he took off to the big city, married him a city girl, and got too much poodle hair up his nose."

I stifle a grin as my side-view mirror reveals Dad rolling his eyes. I turn around and catch Mom biting her lip. My dad, after growing up in Bella Coola, got a scholarship to attend veterinary school in New York City; married Mom, a fellow veterinarian; and ran a dog clinic in a posh part of the "city that never sleeps" before upending our family's life to move back here. In Granddad's eyes, dogs are way, way down the food chain from, say, cattle, horses, and the occasional moose calf.

Granddad hits the brakes and we all lurch forward. "Sorry, gotta piss," he says, swinging the door open and hopping out.

"Really, Daniel. Language," Mom says.

A minute later, Granddad shouts, "Bollocks!"

"What's up, Dad?" My father slips out of the vehicle to join his father, who is studying tracks in a patch of mud. *Dad's a good son*, I reflect. Patient and attentive to Granddad, and so at home here in the West. At home like Mom and I aren't. I tumble out and walk over to where they're standing.

"Plott hounds," the old man mumbles, his sharp green eyes following the tracks until they disappear into the brush. "Pack-hunting devil of a beast. Used by cheating hunter types."

"You're right. We need to report this to Evan Anderson," Dad says.

"Why, is it illegal for hunters to use dogs?" Mom asks, stepping out of the Jeep. "Are there hunters around here? Ray, get back in the Jeep."

"Poachers," Granddad replies. "Killing before the season starts, without licences."

I glance about uneasily, newly alert to the possibility of gun barrels pointed at the four of us from behind devil's-club shrubs. "What kind of poachers?"

Granddad turns his large, somewhat emaciated frame and points a calloused finger at me. "Ever seen a naked bear, grandson?" he demands.

"Uh, no." Like, what else would I answer?

"A bear stripped o' his skin, paws, and gallbladder and left on the mountainsides for the vultures looks eerily like a man," he says.

My stomach goes sour and I just stare at my granddad.

CHAPTER THREE

BACK ON THE ROAD, Granddad is breathing a little raggedly, so I decide to try to distract him.

"So, you know drones aren't just toys. They help search-and-rescue teams find lost hikers, and border patrollers use them to catch undocumented immigrants. In Africa, they're using them to stop elephant poachers."

"Grand," Granddad says.

"They can deliver emergency supplies to disaster zones," Mom contributes. I love that my parents totally support my drone thing.

"Those wee wannabe planes?" Granddad hurls back.

"They help loggers; real estate agents; and oil, gas, and mining companies with surveying," I inform him.

"Damn loggers." Granddad grunts. "Damn real estate agents. Damn oil, gas, and mining bastards. But maybe yer onto something, Ray. Yer a smart boy like yer dad, I know that."

I grin and, glancing in the side-view mirror, catch my dad winking at me.

It has been dark for a couple of hours by the time Mom and Dad have put a cast on the bear's paw, tried and failed to coax him to eat some fruit that Mom mashed up, and finally staked him in the backyard on a chain beside his cage. We've eaten our own supper here in Granddad's log cabin, which we've moved into to help him with what he needs day-to-day. Dad is stoking up the wood stove. Granddad, his shrunken body in droopy green pyjamas, is headed into his bedroom when the phone rings.

Minutes later, Granddad reports, "Evan went up to remove the dead sow and found her body messed with. Paws and gallbladder removed for the black market. They'll investigate more tomorrow."

"What's a gallbladder and why would anyone want that?" I ask, feeding another log onto the fire.

"It's a small organ — a sac the shape of a pear — on the right side of your abdomen, in between your liver and small intestine," Mom explains in effortless vet-speak. "The liver releases bile into the gallbladder for storage before the bile goes on to the small intestine, where it helps with digestion. Some people believe the myth that bear bile is a cure-all for almost anything."

"Myth?" I say.

"Scientists using a Western approach have found no evidence that it works any better than herbs or synthetic bile. Meanwhile, there are evil people who cage young bears and milk it out of them, and kill the older ones to cut it out of them, all for profit." She shakes her head, looking troubled.

"Gross," I say.

"Agreed. When you vomit on an empty stomach, that's bile coming up."

"Seriously TMI, Mom. What about the second cub, Granddad?"

"Gone. No trace. Evan says it's okay to keep this yearling for now, you two being vets," Granddad says, but his tone is disapproving.

"He doesn't know you specialize in poodles," I tease Mom and Dad.

"Shhh." Dad half grins.

"If the cub doesn't eat, he'll weaken and die," Mom says worriedly.

"Yearling, not cub, you stupid city woman," Granddad says.

I'm relieved when Mom ignores him. "Ray, don't you have homework to do?"

"Yeah."

"No letting that bear in to sleep on your bed tonight," Dad instructs with a smile.

"Got it," I say, heading to my room. But later, long after I've done my homework and as soon as the cabin goes quiet, I lean my face against my bedroom's cool windowpane to watch the small grizzly limp to the garage wall, swaying back and forth in the pale moonlight. Guilt twists my gut. He's suffering because of me. I should've just waited things out, not shouted for my trigger-happy granddad.

Tiptoeing into the kitchen, I grab the bowl of mashed fruit Mom brought inside to prevent attracting other animals. Then I take two blankets from the living room sofa before stepping outside.

"Hey, little fellow," I whisper softly, lowering myself into the ratty hammock on our backyard patio, just out of the chain's reach.

The grizzly's ears prick up and his dark eyes turn toward me, searching, considering. His swaying slows. He bawls again.

"I'm sorry you've lost your family. I know how you feel. I'm losing my granddad to cancer. Want some food?" I raise the bowl. The small bear presses his back into the garage wall. I sigh. *You, too*, I think. *I can't save Granddad, or my parents' marriage, or you.* It's hard to please Granddad. And I haven't made any friends here yet. I'm invisible, useless.

"Well, the bowl is here if you want it." I set it on the edge of the patio, wrap myself in the blankets, and settle into the holey hammock. It's definitely not comfy, but the camping trip has clearly tired me, because I'm soon out.

I dream I'm a toddler and my granddad is rocking me to sleep in a hammock in the frigid valley air. Then the old man leans over and grunts like he does, and nuzzles me in the neck. My nose scrunches up at an overpoweringly pungent smell.

Fully awake, I bolt upright.

The bear, dragging his chain, is grunting and snuffling in the weak morning light, sniffing the bowl of food on the patio from afar like an anteater.

Happiness shoots through me.

"Hank," I say softly — on impulse naming him after the puppy in *My Talking Hank*, a mobile game I used to like. The shadow sits up and looks at me warily. "Good boy. Let me help you with that."

Slowly, cautiously, I climb out of my sling, place my hands on either side of the bowl, and crouch there, dead still. I should be scared, and this might be foolish, but he's just a large baby, I remind myself. Besides, I'm the animal whisperer.

My heart skips a beat when the little bear half limps, half waddles over, sticks his nose into the bowl, and slurps up everything in it.

"Good boy. Go to sleep now." I point to his cage, which we've lined with soft rags.

Backing up to the safety of my hammock, I pull my blankets over me again and settle in for another few hours' sleep. My parents won't really care if they find me here in the morning.

What? Hank limps over and rests his nose on my chest, almost overturning the hammock. I completely misjudged the length of that chain! I should be freaked, but I want to cry out with joy. The pressure against my ribs and the watchful, curious eyes warm me. I read no intent of harm in him. He's just lonely, confused. In fact, as he sucks his tongue to the accompaniment of a rumbling sound in his chest, I know instinctively he's purring.

He's going to mend and live!

"You'll be all right," I tell him, battling my nervousness about having a frisky bear so close. Someone who trusts me, sees me, accepts me for who I am. I've finally got a buddy in Bella Coola.

Having grown up learning to read dogs' pain and trauma, I'm fond of animals. Hey, they're easier to relate to than human beings. I begin to hum. Hank closes his eyes. Morning birds break into song. Seated on his haunches, casted paw in his lap, he nestles his muzzle into my neck.

"What? I'm supposed to burp you or tell you a bedtime story? Thought you were a yearling. That's like four and a half in people years, right?"

"Talk to him respectful-like," I remember Granddad saying on the camping trip.

"It's good that you ate, Hank. Let's see. What else can we talk about? Hey, want to hear about the drone models I'm building in my workshop? One is a perfect spying machine the size of a butterfly. The other is my masterpiece: waterproof with thermal capabilities, perfect for flying at night."

"But what are the drones for?" a voice demands.

I sit up, prompting Hank to lift his head off me and drag himself across the patio to his cage.

My next-door neighbour and classmate, Min-jun Kim, is leaning on the half-rotted picket fence between our yards, wearing a worn white terrycloth bathrobe over white pyjamas and rubber boots. He's the short, fit-looking son of a couple that runs a small Korean café in town.

"Yo, Min-jun. Wasn't exactly talking to you. What're you doing up, anyway?"

"Listening to you talk to a bear … who was seriously in the hammock with you?"

I smirk. "He's an orphan with a broken paw. I'm trying to calm him."

"How do you know it's a him?"

"My parents are vets, duh."

Min-jun shivers as a breeze ruffles the legs of his pyjama bottoms.

"How's your grandfather?" he asks.

"He's doing okay."

"Good. Dad's dropping over later to bring some of his special tea. Mr. McLellan needs lots of rest, you know. Helps prevent anxiety and irritation in cancer patients."

"Granddad's been irritable all his life."

Min-jun laughs. "True that. Hey, can I check out your drones sometime?"

"Min—" Crap. My neighbour heard every word I said. "Maybe, but can you just keep that to yourself? No one's supposed to know what I'm making in the workshop."

The Kims moved in two years ago. I don't know them half as well as Granddad does. Can I trust this guy?

"Min-jun Kim!" comes a deep, fiery voice, followed by a mouthful of Korean. A short, muscular man with his shoulders back and chest pushed out appears in Min-jun's backyard, jabbing his finger at my classmate.

Min-jun gives a quick wave and bolts for the back door of his small clapboard house. His glowering father rests beefy arms on the fence top.

"Why is bear in backyard? Is dangerous, yes?"

"Hi, Mr. Kim," I say. "Granddad shot its mother when he thought I was in danger on our camping trip. It has a broken paw, and we're feeding it till it's ready to go back to the wild." Already, I can't imagine parting with the furry creature who rested his head on my chest.

"Hmm," Mr. Kim says with a frown as he studies the sleeping bear. "Be careful, Ray. I come later with tea, like Min-jun say."

Great. Another eavesdropper. I nod. "Thanks."

"Good night."

CHAPTER FOUR

I'M WOLFING DOWN a bowl of oatmeal and telling my parents about my nighttime feeding success (without mentioning that Hank reached the hammock) when the sound of a truck backfiring in our alley makes all three of us jump. I poke my head out to see if Hank might need calming, then freeze at seeing the back gate open, no bear in sight, and the tail end of a dented red pickup truck gunning it down the alley.

"Mom! Dad!" I shout, staring at the still-swinging gate. "Someone just stole Hank!"

I race out and hold up one cut end of his chain. Whoever it was had bolt cutters for sure. I want to scream with panic and anger.

"We have no proof he was actually stolen," Mom insists. "Someone may have cut the chain for a joke, and then he wandered off."

"It's just as well," Granddad says, shrugging. "Wouldn't have lived much longer, here or in the wild, with a no-good paw."

I open my mouth to protest, but Dad says, "You're already late for school, son. We'll keep an eye out, but it's time for you to get gone."

I consider taking off and trying to find Hank instead — but what do I know about tracking an animal? And anyway, my parents can see me on the first part of my half-mile walk to Bella Coola High School.

I drag my feet as I enter the grey wood-clad building. Imagine attending a school without metal detectors at the entrance. One without an aeronautics club, violent gangs, or a shred of fashion sense. In a town with, like, three eating-out places, four stop signs, and no movie theatre or computer store. I so miss New York City! Arlo and Koa keep texting me what they're up to, even sending me photos of the new drones they're building. So jealous they have each other to fly with, consult with, party with.

I make my way to my locker and slump against it, face pressed against its cool metal, heavy heart stalling me there.

"It's the new kid," a tall, black-haired guy passing by whispers in a less-than-friendly tone. All I know is that his name's Cole Thompson and he's a bullying sort of guy. "City-boy dumbass."

Gritting my teeth, I open my locker slowly, gather my books, and walk toward class, all too used to bullies in the big city. But there, *city boy* is not an insult. And after a full month here already, you'd think it would let up. Okay, so what am I doing wrong?

"Seriously?" a girl says in a mocking tone, pointing to the high-tech black jacket I'm wearing. It's the thing in Manhattan right now. I wore it to make an impression. Note to self: wrong impression.

With Hank's kidnapping commandeering my brain, I'm not sure I have the energy to deal with other crap. What is it with these daily insults? Maybe the girl's looking at my black wool beret, tilted to keep my mop of red hair under control, but also to cover my left ear. (My hair used to cover my ear, but I just got a bad haircut.) Or is it the artfully twisted red pashmina scarf, also a thing in the city? I sigh. Maybe my prized silver running shoes? What am I supposed to wear — a flannel shirt, army trousers, and boots?

"Hey, are you gay or just a super nerd?"

"I'm not g—" I start as I swing around in the locker-jammed hallway, but the girl and some jocks scatter with guffaws.

Someone swipes my beret, and my hand flies to my head.

The second of silence that follows pains me more than the insults.

"What? Gross!" says Cole, twirling the cap on his index finger. "You've only got half a left ear!"

"Bike accident," I lie, grabbing at but failing to retrieve the cap. He tosses it to Min-jun, who has just appeared. A group of students gathers.

"Oh. You a hard-core cyclist?" Cole looks almost impressed for a minute.

I shrug, not wanting to push an untruth too far.

"Did you know I'm president of the school Outdoors Club, Ray?" Min-jun asks. "And Cole here is vice-prez. We could use some new blood in the club. Interested in joining?"

I open my mouth to say *no way*, then remember I totally promised myself I'd try to fit in. Anyway, it's not like there are any competing offers on the table. And Min-jun or his dad will tell Granddad I snubbed his invitation.

"Um, sure. Thanks." Then it occurs to me to ask, "What does the Outdoors Club do?" Though I fear I already know.

"You know, we camp, hunt, fish, hike, cycle." Cole squints like he's analyzing every follicle of my reaction.

All the stuff I hate. All in the freakin' scary woods. It's bad enough attending a school whose sports field butts up against bear habitat.

"Excellent. I'd be into that," I say. Maybe I can persuade them to fly drones instead. Min-jun showed some interest last night … er, early this morning. "Hey, if you're into the outdoors, does that mean you know how to track?" I ask the two of them.

Min-jun cocks his head. Cole eyes a good-looking girl passing down the hallway, leaves my beret with Min-jun, and takes off after her. "Maybe. Track what?" Min-jun asks.

"A truck? A bear?" How lame does that sound?

Min-jun laughs. "A truck leaves tire tracks. A bear leaves scat." The kids around us laugh, too.

"My pet grizzly bear, the orphan, got kidnapped this morning, after you left for school." I sound like a total idiot. "Someone in a dented red pickup truck grabbed it. Maybe."

Min-jun looks at me. "Hank? A dented red pickup truck would be the Logan brothers."

"Oh. Where do they live?"

"A farm on the south ridge. I could give you a ride up there on my quad later." He's kind of smiling, like a hunt for a kidnapped bear is the best offer he's had all year.

"Seriously? You mean after school?"

"Sure, why not? I know where you live," my next-door neighbour says, standing like a general with his arms crossed. I'm unsure whether his grin is mocking or friendly.

"You'll get mud-spattered head to toe the way Min-jun drives, so ditch the three-piece suit," some dude jabs.

Three-piece suit? I ignore the guy. "Thanks," I say to Min-jun. I want to ask him why anyone would nab a half-grown bear, but the bell sends everyone scurrying.

"Later," Min-jun says, handing the beret back. "And if you want to make friends here, get rid of the hat, scarf, and jacket, neighbour."

At least he doesn't rule out the designer jeans, shoes, and mesh tee. I sigh and head to class, books pressed tightly against my chest, beret riding on top of them. I stop as a Nuxalk girl, a member of the local First Nation, steps into view just before I reach the classroom. She has a lioness mane of shiny black hair, chestnut eyes, and a tight pink shirt with the words *Drone Chick* on it.

"Drone chick?" I ask, astonished.

"The new kid can read," she says. "What happened to your ear, loser? Looks like someone took a bite out of it."

I whip my beret back on. "A girl got carried away while kissing it."

"Ha ha." She whirls around to walk into class, but I touch her elbow. "I'm Ray McLellan. Do you fly drones? I'm totally into drones."

"I heard. You're the taxidermist's grandson. How's your grandfather?" Her voice is neutral.

"Doing okay, thanks." I'm not about to say *dying*, since I guess everyone in town knows that already.

"Dorothy Dawson," she says stiffly. "Yes, my father and I are into UASs. So if you need any parts or repairs, let us know." This cute girl who knows about unmanned aerial systems then marches into class and takes a seat near the students who hassled me earlier.

Trying to shake off the sense that everyone is staring at me, measuring me, and finding me lacking in whatever traits allow one a free pass into Bella Coola cooldom, I look around for an empty desk. Min-jun is seated at the back of the room.

I slide into the seat beside him. "Hey."

"Math." He groans dramatically. "I prefer phys. ed."

"I prefer math," I inform him. Though if I want to fit in, I remind myself, I need to remember to do my best in gym and hide my smarts in other classes.

"Good morning, class," says Mr. Mussett. "So, yesterday the assignment was to form a word problem that demonstrates the usefulness of math. Ray, please read yours first."

I shrug, glad I found the homework easy.

"Ahem. After removing your cap, McLellan," Mr. Mussett says.

I try to shift my scarf up to my left ear as I pull my beret off and plop it on my desk. A few intakes of breath behind me indicate my scarf hasn't done the job.

"Oh," said Mr. Mussett, reddening. "Sorry."

Defiantly, I whip off my scarf.

"Gross," someone says under her breath. Someone who apparently hasn't heard about my damaged ear already.

"A mountain lion bit it off," I lie, loudly enough for everyone to hear, an announcement rewarded by a low mumble of voices. "Here's my word problem: A search-and-rescue officer is attempting to find lost hikers with his drone. His two-pound machine accelerates straight upwards — droners would say 'throttles up' — at two-point-two-five metres per second squared, until it's above the trees. Determine how much time it will now take for the drone to travel forward one hundred and sixty-five metres to a clearing where the hikers are waiting, the drone continuing to travel forward at the same speed, of course."

Most kids furrow their eyebrows like I've just spoken Chinese. A few eye me curiously. Dorothy raises her hand.

"Yes, Dorothy," Mr. Mussett says.

"But as soon as the drone is above the trees, the wind will throw it off, so there's no way it can maintain two-point-two-five metres per second squared," she says in a confident tone.

"Ray?" Mr. Mussett asks, looking like he's not sure how to tackle her objection himself.

"Most up-to-date drones — at least the one that I'm designing — have a strong stabilization system built in that won't allow for significant drift to throw them off," I respond, with what I hope is a friendly glance at my fellow droner. "So it's just math."

"Just math," someone mimics.

"Smartass," says someone else.

Dorothy is absorbed in pressing the lead tip of her pencil into her desktop with such force it breaks. "What's really with your ear?" she demands under her breath.

"Signifies membership in a prestigious New York City gang," I lie.

She raises her eyebrows. I hope it means she might sit next to me at lunchtime.

Four classes later — plus one lonely lunch hour, seven more ear comments, and a chilly trudge home — I collapse into an easy chair in the living room across from my blanket-wrapped granddad. He's snoring by the wood stove under the cold, glassy stares of one deer, one elk, one mountain goat, and one black bear head, all mounted on the walls. It's way weird living in a taxidermist's house. And it definitely doesn't feel like home yet.

I hear my parents arguing in the house's spacious former verandah, long ago converted to a bright room and now outfitted as the town's new animal clinic. The previous vet retired a year ago from some decrepit digs up the street. At first my parents were going to rent a place they could use as a clinic, but soon after we moved, I overheard Mom tell Dad, "We may not be here long, depending on how your father does, so let's not get too committed and settled in this town."

"'This town' is our new home, dear," Dad replied stiffly. "It's where I grew up, where I've always dreamed of returning someday. You agreed to give it a try. And having the outdoors so close at hand is perfect for a boy of Ray's age."

"A boy of his age, maybe, but not Ray himself," she said coldly before walking away from his attempted hug.

Sighing, I glance out at the backyard patio, where Hank's dirty pawprints are still visible. My throat catches as I gaze at the empty feeding bowl I set on the kitchen counter that morning.

"Where are you, Hank?" I whisper. Closing my eyes, I imagine letting the bear into the living room and allowing him to climb clumsily into my lap. The image melts the humiliations of the school day and makes my parents' raised voices go away. My left ear vibrates only slightly when I imagine Hank lifting a paw to it, as if he's just noticed his master is disfigured. Something the whole school discovered today.

"Bejesus. When did you get home?" Granddad asks, eyelids lifting as he stirs in his chair.

"Just now. Hear anything about the cub?"

"Yearling, not cub. No, the smelly thing's wandered back to the woods, I s'pose. I take no stock in yer conspiracy theory o' kidnapping, by the way. Some hooligans probably cut the chain just for fun in the night."

I grit my teeth, not in the mood to argue. "How are you?"

"Still this side of the green grass. How was school?"

"Great. Made lots of new friends and joined the Outdoors Club." Reclosing my eyes, I try to hang onto the imagined sensation of Hank on my lap, his heart beating right through my tee.

"About time."

"Min-jun invited me to join. He's president."

"'Course he is. He's athletic and knows his outdoors."

Pretending I don't get the hint, I say, "Fetch you some tea, Granddad?"

"With a dollop o' whiskey if yer mum ain't around."

"Does Mr. Kim's tea help you?"

"Nope. Doctor's pills do better. But don't say it, 'cause I like his visits."

"Of course. I'll get you tea. Mom and Dad are in the clinic." Even a half-deaf senior citizen can surely hear the heated arguing and the dog yelping in the clinic.

"Did Mom and Dad look more for Hank?" I ask Granddad. "Notify police and stuff?"

"Who's Hank?" Granddad replies with a snort.

A sharp rap sounds at the back door, and Mr. Kim walks in with a tray holding a steaming cup. Awesome timing. Now I don't have to get up to make Granddad tea.

"Is healthy," says the jowled man with sprinkles of grey in his black hair. He puts the tray down beside Granddad and helps himself to a seat on the dusty sofa.

I examine leafy bits floating at the top of the mug and lean closer to sniff the bitter-smelling drink. But I stop myself from wrinkling my nose as I hand it to Granddad.

"Did you see the yearling while I was at school, Mr. Kim? Or talk to anyone who has?"

Mr. Kim shoots me a look. "No, Ray. Wild animal no belong in town, anyway."

"You tell 'im," Granddad says, lifting his teacup like he's making a toast. "How's life, Jae-bum?"

Mr. Kim's real first name is Jae-beom.

"I better than you," Mr. Kim says, putting down his tea before leaning over his neighbour to pull up the blanket that has slipped from around the old man's neck. Then he stands to stoke up the wood stove.

"Yeah, well, I'm still better looking," Granddad shoots back.

"Have it your way." Mr. Kim smiles. "My wife make you kimchee for vitamin. Min-jun bring later. He do homework because Ray impress him today."

"At school work or sports?" Granddad asks. As if he cares about the first.

"Math. Min-jun very good at sports," Mr. Kim asserts in his deep voice.

"Ray, you've been here a month already," Granddad says, face creased in disapproval. "Which sports teams have you joined?"

"The drone-flying team," I deadpan.

"Stop yer pussyfooting," the old man says. "At least he's joined the Outdoors Club," he boasts to Mr. Kim.

"Min-jun tell me. Have outdoor club in New York?"

"Ha!" I respond. "The outdoors in New York City is where the drug sellers, gangs, and muggers hang out. Dodging them is a world-class sport. But some drone pilots and I would take over a corner of Central Park on Saturdays." Inside my school back there, the only thing that ever interested me was drone-building in shop class. Sports? Give me a break.

"I met a girl today who flies drones," I inform Granddad while checking my watch and reminding myself that Min-jun will arrive soon for the quad ride.

"Stay clear o' Dorothy Dawson," Granddad replies.

How'd he know her name? Can he read my mind? "Huh? Why?"

"Her father was in the military, and he's off his rocker a wee bit."

"What does that mean?"

A crash, scream, and howl make all three of us look toward the door leading to the former porch.

"Begorrah!" my granddad says.

"Ray!" comes my mother's voice. "Help! Now!"

CHAPTER FIVE

WITH MR. KIM on my heels, I fling open the clinic door to see a large golden retriever hanging half off the operating table and an intravenous pole teetering above it. My mother is on her back on the white-tiled floor, surrounded by glass shards and blood. My father is squatting on the floor beside her, one arm pressing a wad of blood-soaked gauze against her arm, another raised to prevent the half-conscious dog from falling on them.

"I've got him!" I shout, dragging the dog back onto the table, hands well away from its snapping mouth.

"He came to too early," Mom says. "He tried to bite me."

"Your mother backed up and knocked a beaker off the counter, then slipped and fell on the shards," Dad says. "Son, if the patient is stabilized, please hand me the bottle of hydrogen peroxide." Dad likes to call every creature we work on a patient rather than an animal.

I grab the bottle that will disinfect my mother's cut and hand it to Dad, wincing at the sight of blood stains on Mom's white lab coat.

"I can drive you to hospital," Mr. Kim offers, taking a muzzle he spots hanging from a wall hook and slapping it on the retriever's mouth. I wince. *The guy seems totally unfazed by the half-awake growling, drooling, jerking retriever*, I think, as he pulls the straps of the plastic-cup-like device tight. Very tight.

"Never mind, Sean," Mom protests. "I'm fine. And thanks for the offer, Jae, but I don't need a hospital. I need to get that drip going again."

"Ray can do it, honey," Dad says, continuing to dab the hydrogen peroxide on her wounds.

"I've got it," I declare, not wanting the dog to feel pain or cause more chaos.

I check the medication bag hanging from the pole, making sure the point of the fluid chamber tube goes into the large port and the flow tap wheel is in the stop position. I step over to the sink to wash my hands with antibacterial soap and then position myself to gently turn the muzzled patient back onto his stomach.

Next, I apply a tight wrap, extend the dog's foreleg, and identify its cephalic vein. My parents, of course, have already clipped away fur from the site and sterilized it. The vein is in clear view under the skin. Removing the IV's cap and loosening the catheter, I expose the needle, recap it, and press my thumb down beside the vein so it won't move while I insert the needle. Perfect. From the corner of my eye, I see Mr. Kim staring at me in astonishment as I take the catheter out of the cap, face the needle hole up, and insert it at a forty-five-degree angle into the vein.

As blood enters the hub, I smile, apply thumb pressure, secure the IV, and adjust the flow.

The dog sighs as if in relief, slipping back into sleep, ready now for his surgery.

"Thanks, Ray," Mom says as she's pulled to her feet by Dad. "How was school?"

"Good."

Outside, an engine sputters and roars. The high-pitched honk of Min-jun's quad makes everyone turn toward the window. My parents look from the figure sitting on the ATV to me.

"Hey, Mom, Dad. Min-jun offered me a ride. Okay?"

"You and Min-jun are friends?" Mom fails to hide a slight frown as she straightens up beside her fully anes-thetized patient. Most mothers would be happy about a first friend in a new school, especially a next-door neighbour they sort of know, but I can see her measuring how that weakens her bargaining power on the return-to-New-York campaign.

"Min-jun is good driver," Mr. Kim says.

"Okay. Be back for supper," Dad calls out as I grab my backpack and pass Mr. Kim and Granddad to step out the front door.

"He'll be back in five minutes after falling off that rust bucket," Granddad announces loudly enough for every-one, including Min-jun, to hear. "Sean, is yer wife done making all that bloody racket on the porch? Saints preserve us! Can't get me an afternoon nap around here no-how."

"Sorry about Granddad," I say, staring at Min-jun's mud-spattered machine, which looks like a wannabe army jeep on its fourth tour of war.

Min-jun laughs. "He's our official valley grump, but with a good heart. Hey, like my stripped-down two-up? A little tippy on sharp corners, but lots of snap for a fifty horsepower."

I have no idea what he has just said, but I give him a thumb's up.

"You're joking about the bear kidnapping, right?" he asks.

As I lead him behind the house for a look, I give him a quick rundown of events.

"A set of four off-road traction tires stopped, then squealed off here, for sure," Min-jun says, studying the dirt alley beside our back gate. "Did you see them load the bear in? Catch a licence plate number?"

"No," I admit.

He crosses the lane and examines the grass and bushes leading up the hill. "No sign of a young grizzly here recently, not that I'm an expert. It's possible he got shoved into the pickup truck. But why anyone around here would want a —"

"Is it okay if we ride up to the Logan brothers' place, then? The ones you said have a dented red pickup truck?"

He hesitates. "Sure, whatever. But don't go accusing them or anything. Not the kind of guys you want to mess with." He shows me where to climb into a small sitting space behind him. It has a wimpy backrest and side bars to hold onto. The noise and jerk of the take-off make me panic-grip the bars. Having exchanged my beret for my dad's New York Yankees cap, I clamp a hand on it to keep it from flying off, nearly bouncing off the vehicle in the process.

We bump along Bella Coola's potholed roads, then leave town, heading up into the mountains on a steep dirt track. Ten minutes later, a high fence with a barbed-wire gate and two giant padlocks blocks us. Min-jun applies the brakes in the choking dust.

"I've been here before to buy firewood, and it was locked then, too. Oh well, we tried." He starts to turn his ATV around, but I lay a hand on his shoulder till he switches off the ignition. I scan the big, dusty property. The faded ranch house is surrounded by rusted farm equipment, a collapsing barn, and a collection of weed-infested wrecked cars. No animals or crops in sight.

"That's the one," I say, pointing to a beat-up Ford pickup truck parked in front of the house. I leap off the quad.

"Hello! Anyone home?" I shout. "Hmm, we need to climb the fence and search around for Hank."

"We? Not me, dude. And not you unless you have a bulletproof jacket," Min-jun says.

Telling myself he's joking, I search for footholds in the fence but don't find any. And the barbed wire on top of the gate would wreck my best jeans for sure.

"Let's walk around the place at least," I suggest.

"What?" Min-jun screws up his face, then shrugs and parks his ride off the road, behind some bushes. We're a third of the way around the fence, close to the barn, when two large, snarling dogs tear out of the farmhouse straight for us, crashing into the fence and leaping up, saliva running down their chin.

"What the —" Min-jun backs up. "What if they jump this fence and maul us?"

The Plott hounds are making such a racket that it sets off more dogs in the barn.

"Not going to happen," I say, drawing myself up to my full height. "No!" I instruct our would-be attackers in a deep leader-of-the-pack voice. "Go home. Now!"

Min-jun looks astonished as the sleek hunting dogs with bulldog-like brindle coats take their paws off the fence, observe me for a minute or two, then trot silently back to the house.

"Hank?" I call toward the barn.

Maybe it's wishful thinking, but I swear I hear his cry from inside.

Then, for the second time in twenty-four hours, a shotgun blast rips through the air beside me. Min-jun disappears in a zigzagging sprint toward his stashed vehicle. I'm about to follow when a man appears from the barn and walks to within feet of the fence.

"Who the hell're you, and what're ya doin' 'ere?" A pinched-faced, fortysomething guy with a full beard and moustache approaches, holding a hunting rifle. He's wearing a tan vest covered in ominously bulging pockets over a black-and-red checkered flannel shirt, camo pants, and army boots. Real-man Bella Coola fashion.

"Hey," I manage to say through a tight throat. "I'm Ray, Daniel McLellan's grandson. Just moved to Bella Coola with my parents, the veterinarians. Been hiking and I'm lost, I guess. Sorry if I upset your dogs. Can you point me toward the road to town, please?"

"There's only one road, idiot. Now git 'fore I let all my dogs out," he says in a gruff voice.

"Nice hounds," I say. "They're what, about three? And that one's expecting soon."

The man frowns as he looks from me to the dog I'm pointing to.

"Shiny coats, lean bodies, and healthy gums. Guess we won't be seeing them in our clinic anytime soon. But you know we're there if you need us. Have a great day." I tip the right side of my baseball cap to him so that the left side still hides my ear.

"Out!" he shouts, shaking his gun. "We don't need an effing vet. I'm the vet 'ere. Went to high school wi' your dad, by the way. And ya don't recognize me, do ya?" The tone is scathing, like he and my father were never really best buddies, which wouldn't surprise me somehow.

"Oh," I say, surprised. "We've met? Probably when I was younger, here on vacation." Maybe before he grew that moustache and beard that hide most of his face?

"Out!" he repeats, and I can tell he means it.

Adrenalin pumping, I nod and back away a bit before turning to hurry to the quad.

"You're full of it, but you've got nerve," Min-jun informs me, shaking his head and waiting for me to climb into his back saddle. "That was Oakley, the older brother. He has a younger brother, Orion. Both are bad news. Did you seriously tell him his dogs have healthy gums? Okay, dog dentist, let's dip. If those two have your cub, it'll be a bear rug by tomorrow."

Bear rug? I turn away so he won't see me wince. "You knew they were like that but brought me up here anyway?"

He shrugs and smirks. "Your initiation, new boy."

So I've been played. Or so he thinks. I bite my tongue. "Well, we're not done yet." I pull Bug and his controller out of my backpack. "We're going to stay behind this bush but get a close-up of what they're up to."

Min-jun's eyes widen and he blinks a few times, then leans forward. "Your funeral," he says, staring at my little 'copter.

Ten minutes later, I say, "Do you want to try the first-person-view goggles?" I fit the FPV goggles on his head. That way he can see what Bug's camera is seeing at the same time I can on my less-clear mini-tablet.

"Frickin' amazing," he mutters as I launch the drone up to a bird's-eye view of the farm. "Oakley's using a mini-vac on the back of their truck. Orion's holding his nose like whatever they're vacuuming up stinks. How come they don't hear this thing over their heads and shoot it out of the sky?"

"Vacuum cleaner's noise, I guess." I veer my machine toward the barn and in through one of its glassless windows.

"Hey! Did you see that dog jump up and almost bite it?" Cole says.

"Yeah, thinks it's a Frisbee or something."

"Okay, okay, Ray, you're making me dizzy spinning around inside like that. Why are you hovering over that big dog cage? Hey, no bear in the place, bro. Just another pack of dogs ready to eat us alive."

"Not just any pack of dogs, Min-jun. Plott hounds." I fly my drone back through the open window and to base.

"Who?"

"Bear-hunting dogs."

"Oh. How would an uptight city boy know that?"

"My grumpy granddad. And who says I'm uptight?" I punch him lightly in the shoulder. He whips off the goggles, a grin stretched wide above his dimpled chin, and punches me back as my drone settles neatly on the patch of ground beside us.

"You're right," I tell him, folding up Bug and returning him to my backpack. I climb into my quad seat. "We didn't see Hank. But he's there, or was. I swear I saw some of his hair in the back of the truck. I'll put the conservation officer guy onto them tonight and maybe have Hank home by morning." Yeah, a part of me knows Hank might not be here, might even be dead, but I'm way too stubborn and optimistic to let that thought win.

"Officer Anderson?" Min-jun says doubtfully. "Maybe." He fires up the quad.

"I owe you, Min-jun. Like maybe a pizza tomorrow? Does Bella Coola have a decent pizzeria?"

My driver spins his machine around as tightly as a mob getaway vehicle. "Any more smartass questions like that and I'll push the rear-seat ejection button. Hang on or —"

Luckily, my palms are already wrapped around the support bars, and the valley wind blows away the rest of his words.

CHAPTER SIX

HANK'S NOT BACK by morning — it's a professional development day, which gives us a break from school — but I call Officer Anderson, and the conservation officer says he's on it. My entire body sags with happy relief, until I realize Granddad overheard me and knows what's up.

"Kidnapped by the Logans?" He shakes his head and points a trembling finger at me. "Yer a right eejit" — that's Irish for *idiot* — "with a wild imagination, grandson, raising a stink for naught! I reckon yer mother has let you watch too many crime movies. The thing got cut loose and then just wandered off, like they do. It's good riddance to the yard-crapping little beastie anyway. How dare you phone my friend Evan Anderson!"

But if I'd asked the old man first … I slink away from Granddad's temper with guilty confusion.

My dad sticks his head into the living room from the clinic. "You ran into Oakley Logan? We were in the same class. Were so-so friends. We both wanted to be veterinarians."

"But?" I prompt.

Dad shrugs. "He didn't have the grades or money. Worked in the previous vet's office for a while as an untrained assistant. I've tried to have coffee with him since we moved here, but he seems to have a chip on his shoulder."

"Jealous," Mom suggests as I move into the clinic and watch her mending a young dachshund torn up last night by a cornered raccoon. "There are rough-and-tough hicks around here," she adds. "Can you hand me the scalpel, Sean?"

"Don't you need a hemostat first? He's —"

Does Bella Coola know how lucky it is to have two first-class vets?

I contemplate Dad growing up here, and how his enthusiasm for the place showed whenever we were here on vacation. He was always trying to pass along knowledge and a love of nature to me in a gentle way, not like Granddad's be-an-outdoorsman-or-else approach.

On my thirteenth birthday, Dad gave me a camera, then took me to the Belarko bear-viewing platform along the Atnarko River in Tweedsmuir Provincial Park, about forty-five minutes east of Bella Coola. Surrounded by electric fencing and staffed by BC Parks staff and volunteers from the Nuxalk Nation, it was a zone where we could see and photograph bears as they dove and splashed in the river, played with their cubs, and caught and ate salmon.

"Look," Dad whispered, pointing.

We could hear the moms grunting at their babies, watch the youths wrestle each other playfully, and marvel at how nimbly the cubs climbed trees. I lifted my camera and clicked away. We weren't allowed to talk, or move quickly, or make any noise. We could only whisper as we watched the great creatures, in awe.

The rangers at the platform seemed to know every visiting grizzly by name: Bent Ear, Lady Diver, Y-Bear, and the Rowdy Twins, for instance. I watched Bent Ear for a long time, wondering if his appendage buzzed and roared when memories of whatever trauma caused it came back to him. I wondered if he tried to hide his disfigured ear, and whether sows were attracted to or repelled by it.

"That's one of our largest, a male," the ranger whispered to us, pointing to a furry creature standing on his hind legs that made me shrink back, shuddering. "Six hundred kilograms, or thirteen hundred pounds. Ten feet tall when he stands up like that."

I backed up involuntarily as the park ranger kept talking. Dad smiled reassuringly. Later, we watched one mother grizzly dip a quick paw into the river, bring up a three-foot-long pink-tinged forty-pound Chinook salmon, and squeeze till the eggs squirted out like jelly from a doughnut right into her waiting mouth. Then she licked up every spilled egg from the nearby rocks and tossed the rest of the salmon away like it was a useless wrapper. Dad and I chuckled together, holding hands.

"Look how much she's wasting," I objected.

Dad grinned. "They do that only in the height of the salmon season. When there are fewer fish, they eat everything. Sometimes twelve salmon a day, the equivalent of thirty burgers. But the eggs and brains are the most nutritious, and they need to fatten up to survive the winter."

"Yeah, they get so fat they have to dig belly-sized holes to lie down comfortably," I said, remembering something I'd read. I pictured them like kids on a sandy beach.

"That's right," the ranger whispered, winking at Dad. "And in the early spring, it's the opposite. They're thin, hungry, and cranky."

Now, I think sadly, *it's Granddad who's thin and cranky, and his only son has rushed to Bella Coola to care for him.* I respect that, even if I miss New York City.

I head outside and cross the yard to unlock the large padlock on Granddad's workshop. I stride into the back room of the workshop. Granddad hasn't kicked me out of it since I sort of claimed it as my own.

Drone batteries line one scrubbed-down shelf. My soldering iron, wires, screwdrivers, tapes, and zip ties are piled up on another. On the back wall above the shelf are drone diagrams and Federal Aviation Administration and Transport Canada posters of UASs. I've moved stacks of Granddad's yellowed hunting magazines off the floor to make room for a table with an iron clamp to do my soldering. My two projects in progress sit on the workbench, like Pinocchio puppets awaiting a wand. Or, more like, waiting for me to insert parts from a mail-order package that arrived yesterday.

I pull up a grimy swivel chair and breathe in the space's peace and quiet. Working on my drones awhile will distract me from thinking about Hank. All this Officer Anderson needs to do is show up at the Logan farm, search their barn, and find Hank wherever those guys have hidden him. The brothers can't let dogs loose on a conservation officer. Anderson can gently load the bear into his official truck and drive it back down the mountain to us. *Hank will be home in hours*, I tell myself. Anderson will allow him to stay here because we're vets, and Mom and Dad will let Hank hang around till he's healed. Granddad will mumble an apology (yeah, right). Optimistic, for sure, but I'd rather be an optimist than think about the alternatives. Meanwhile, I'll put in some time here, in my family-combat escape bunker.

First, I pull out the infrared thermal sensor that came by mail yesterday, my heart beating fast. My thermal unmanned aerial vehicle, or UAV, a.k.a. Skyliner, is nearly complete, just missing a few final touches. I'm especially excited about his underbelly custom pick-up hook, kind of like one of those claws that pick up stuffed toys from a two-dollar-a-play vending machine. The hook can't carry much weight, only about a can of soda, but hey, it's way cool anyway, especially given the drone's ability to see in the dark. Yeah! Skyliner's like a bat that can fly with a fig or grasshopper in its grip. For now, he'll work with my smaller batteries, but I'll need to make improvements if I want this baby to fly the thirty minutes he could. I make some quick modifications to the thermal sensor with my screwdriver, strap in a few wires, and click the hook into place underneath the belly of the beast on the gimbal. Skyliner is going to be perfect for spying at night.

Next I lift up my smaller, palm-sized drone, a.k.a. Butterfly. "You, little monarch, are going to be my perfect daytime spy in the sky. Just need to figure out how to power your on-board computer chip without draining the batteries too much."

I set her down delicately and tinker for a few minutes until I punch in enough power for the computer. (I have no idea why I consider Skyliner and Bug males and Butterfly a female. But I'm the dad, right?)

Since Butterfly is now ready for a test phase, I grab the remote, take the tiny drone outside, and find a clearing to launch her. She does well at first, gliding swiftly through the air like a hummingbird on a beautiful spring day. Then the breeze picks up and Butterfly starts beeping. Damn. The on-board computer is losing connection with my controller! She drifts back and forth, then tilts and descends directly into a heap of Hank's day-old scat. My shoulders droop and my nose scrunches as I lift her out with pinched fingers. After brushing off the reminder of Hank in the grass, I scan the surrounding slopes.

"Hank!" I call out. And more softly, "Hank?"

The rustle of trees, the slap of waves on the nearby river, and the pip-pip of an eagle high above are my only replies. I sigh and kick a rock. It's too quiet here. I miss the din of honking cars, squealing tires, and creaking construction cranes, the blur of yellow taxis, bicycle couriers, and cop cars.

Or do I? I guess it's just what I was used to — the rhythms of city life. Sixteen years of it, minus our annual vacations here. And mostly what I remember of vacations in Bella Coola is same-old: trying to keep my head low as Granddad verbally slaps Mom around and alternately bosses, encourages, and shakes his head hopelessly at me. Dad is never in the line of fire, but he makes for a weak ref.

Only because he's so patient and loves all three of us alike.

We've landed here like tourists trying to steer a Central Park rental boat with a broken oar, spinning, arguing, getting nowhere. We need to pull together somehow.

Yes, I miss Arlo and Koa and New York City a lot. How dare Dad tear us away with so little notice, especially in the middle of a school year? I'm totally pissed about that. *But Granddad is dying,* I keep reminding myself. Dad wants to be near him while he still can, and to help. He's thoughtful and loyal that way. Besides, I don't want to be obsessed with missing the city like Mom. Her homesickness is tearing us apart. No, this isn't home yet. But it was, for just a moment, when Mom, Dad, and I bonded over Hank. All the more reason to find him and get him back here. If someone has kidnapped him, they haven't killed him. I refuse to believe it.

Lifting Butterfly, I examine her sensor and shell to see if there's any damage. "If Officer Anderson doesn't find Hank, you will," I tell her. I contemplate what she needs. Maybe I should resolder some of the connections.

The gimbal is now damaged, so I'll have to order a few bits to repair that. Eventually, I return to the workshop and line up my parts to repair what I can for the moment. The parts for the rest should take only a week to arrive, after which my drone fleet — Bug, Butterfly, and Skyliner — will be complete.

I set Butterfly down and rifle through the room's warped wooden drawers. A fish hook pokes me in the thumb. A broken hammer head greets me like a two-headed slug. A jar holds corroded coins that look old enough to be worth something on eBay. A damp, ancient phone book features a photo of Bella Coola in pioneer days. In other words, pretty much like it looks now.

"If you need any parts or repairs, let us know." Did Dorothy Dawson really say that the other day? Imagine Bella Coola having a drone chick! I page through the old phone book looking for *Dawson*, coughing as mouse turds spill out from the mouldy pages. It lists a MacKenzie Dawson. Her dad? I punch the number into my phone.

Holding my damaged Butterfly in one palm, my phone in the other, I feel my pulse rise. What exactly does Dorothy have in her workshop? So many parts she can actually sell stuff on the side? To whom, and why? Or was she inviting me around to get to know me better? Well, I need a gimbal, and a guy's got to check out his local UAV supplier at some point.

"Dorothy. It's —"

"Hi, Ray. I have call display." It's her same impatient school voice.

"Um, you said you had some drone parts and I was wondering if you might have a gimbal I could buy." My hand's sweating and I sound like I'm mumbling.

There's a sigh, like I'm interrupting very important work. "For a custom UAV or just some toy?"

"Uh —" I'm pissed now, but I don't dare show it. "Custom, duh."

She utters her street address in the monotone of a bored secretary. "In the garage behind the house," she finishes.

"Biatch," I whisper after I think she has hung up.

"I heard that," she says icily. With a click, the line goes dead.

My face warm, I stomp out of the workshop toward the house.

"Mom, Dad," I call into the clinic.

But their voices are too loud for them to hear mine.

"This dog is not going to … The wound is —"

"Darling, we have to —"

"Ray, grandson," comes Granddad's voice from the living room, "no bear delivery yet. But I'm pretty sure you've put yerself on the Logan hit list, which means my ass is grass for future taxidermy orders from them. I'm inclined to mount yer head if you don't —"

"I'm off to the Dawsons' for a drone part," I call out, in case any of the three care.

The simple green rancher, in need of a paint job, sits on a modest plot of land in need of weeding and mowing.

Bypassing the house, I step along cracked, tilted slabs of pavement to the side door of a tall garage.

As I lift my hand to knock, I hear a small dog's high-pitched barking, then a click and the sliding of a heavy bolt. The door opens a crack to reveal a Nuxalk man with squared shoulders and a fierce look. He's wearing a white lab coat and spit-and-polish black shoes. At his knees is a well-clipped, cream-coloured miniature poodle in a pink leather collar. The dog gives a half-hearted bark accompanied by vigorous tail wagging.

I bend down to read the name tag on the poodle's collar and pat the head of tight curls. "Hi, Pilot." Then I stand and offer my hand to the man. "Mr. Dawson? I'm —"

"Daniel McLellan's grandson," he finishes for me in a suspicious tone, looking me over like I'm a faulty used drone for sale, and continuing to hold the door half-closed. "Dorothy, it's a civilian seeking entrance to our facility."

"It's okay, Dad. He just needs a part," she says in a patient tone. Over Mr. Dawson's shoulder, I can see that she's standing at the top of a stepladder, arranging things on a high shelf. The poodle trots to a dog basket near the foot of the ladder and lies down. "Good girl, Pilot," Dorothy says.

"A part for what?" Mr. Dawson demands.

"A drone," I answer. "I called before —"

"It's okay, Dad," Dorothy repeats in a docile voice that makes me wonder if it's really her speaking. "He's cleared for access."

Cleared for access? The door opens wide enough for me to step in, and Dorothy's dad backs away slowly, his expression wary. As he closes the door firmly behind me and pushes a black button on the wall that slides a red iron bolt back into place, I notice a beribboned military uniform hanging stiffly from a hook on the back of the door. I figure it has been a while since its brass buttons could close around Mr. Dawson's middle.

More impressive are the high, warehouse-style surround of shelves and tool racks over several workbenches and the ceiling covered in fluorescent lights lit up like we're in a baseball stadium. Unlike my workshop, with its organized chaos, this one is squeaky clean and stacked to capacity with oscilloscopes, battery chargers, giant gimbals, high-end thermal and zoom cameras, even a 3-D printer. In amazement, I turn to take in more: shelves of drone motors, radios, spare propellers and other parts in cellophane boxes, receivers, and a neatly organized desk with a giant computer underneath and three wall-mounted screens above it. The booming Bluetooth speakers on each side look like they could pack a punch.

"What is this, Area 51?" I try to joke. Seriously, it's like a secret wing of a UAS. Or winglet, anyway.

"It's our garage," Dorothy replies dryly, finally turning from her shelving activities like a librarian who has just noticed a patron. "Dad used to work on drones for Joint Task Force 2, one of Canada's special operations units, and we still, um —"

"— indulge in it as a hobby." Mr. Dawson completes the sentence while giving his daughter a stern look.

"Right," I say, sweating under the bright lights, focused on the poodle thumping her small tail. She's a few months old, her paws still oversized compared to her tiny body.

"How big is your drone?" Dorothy asks, all businesslike, her tone beginning to feel like jabs from the tools on the bench below her. She climbs nimbly down the ladder to land on the polished cement floor. She's wearing a black skirt and tights with a pink sweater, and her thick hair is tied back with a pink ribbon. Seriously, she looks like she's about to head off to a party.

She looks at my drone with feigned disinterest, opens and closes some drawers, and narrows it down to one part, which she presents in open palms.

"That one should work," I say. "Want to go outside to test the drone with me, in case it might, um, need something else?" I sound like a total idiot, but the lights and lack of welcome are getting to me, like I'm a visitor to a high-security prison.

"Sure," she answers, so quickly I'm taken aback. "Be right back, Dad," she says gently, like a mother reassuring a child. And she strides over to press the black button that unlocks the door. Pilot leaps up and trots after us.

"High security," I kid her as the door closes behind us and I breathe more easily in the gone-to-seed yard.

She shrugs. "He's military."

"Retired," I venture.

"Tell *him* that."

"How long have you been into drones?"

She examines her pink polished fingernails. "Since my mother died two years ago."

"Oh. I'm sorry." I pat Pilot's head, then lift an earflap instinctively. No dirt or wax.

Dorothy heaves a deep sigh, then glances sideways at me, evaluating me in some way. "Mom died of cancer. Her last words were to take care of Dad, and since this is where he spends all his time, it's what I do, too."

Her tone is soft and sad, and her chin rests on her chest. Some crazy part of me wants to reach over and touch her reassuringly. Then she lifts her head, and the moment is over. She's all business when she points to Butterfly. "How'd you damage your gimbal?"

I hand the drone to her. "Fell into bear crap."

Her shiny fingernails loosen their hold on Butterfly for a moment, then she bends down, wipes the drone on the straw-like lawn, and laughs. "Your pet bear's scat? The cub I heard you nearly got shot trying to find at the Logans'?"

How did she hear that already? "His name is Hank, and my drones are going to find him if the conservation officer doesn't."

She shakes her head and half smiles, which is an improvement in our shaky relations, at least. "How long have you been droning?"

"According to my granddad, I've been droning on and on since I was born."

Her smile widens as she cocks her head. "And that would be a compliment from Mr. McLellan."

"I got into it through a club at school two years ago. I like designing and constructing them as much as flying them."

She takes the piece from my hand. "Like my dad," she mumbles. "Spends all our money on parts. Thinks he's going to build the mother of all drones, maybe earn more chest candy from the government."

"Chest candy?"

"Ribbons and medals," she says a little impatiently. "You should be able to attach the camera to the gimbal without having to solder anything. If I insert it here like this, it'll …"

She places Butterfly on the ground, grabs my remote control, and, before I can say a word, flicks the joystick. Butterfly launches off the ground, humming higher and higher into the sky. Then, without warning, Dorothy pushes the controller back into my hands, reaches into her skirt pocket, and pulls out a controller and small cherry-red custom drone of her own.

"Duel ya," she says.

I grin.

She launches hers, and we line them up in the air to perform an acrobatic aerial show for all and none to see. Up toward the clouds, down toward the lawn, around and around, like a pair of well-coordinated dancers. Finally, I begin to slow my drone down, lining it up for a race. She sees my move and lowers her drone beside Butterfly.

"Three. Two —"

In an instant we're off, both too excited to wait for the full countdown. Swooping and twirling through the air, our drones whirl through the valley, dipping between trees. Eventually, I let her pull ahead, watching her little guy admiringly.

"Ha! I won," she declares.

"You did," I agree, letting Butterfly rejoin hers as we hover near the frisky spring river.

"Second Lieutenant Dawson!" comes a shout from the garage door. "Leave the civilian and march your ass right back in here."

"Yes, General," she calls back effortlessly, soothingly. She turns to me. "That'll be sixty-five dollars," she says cheerfully.

I dig out my wallet and dish out the cash, even if the price is ridiculously steep.

"Dismissed, Civilian McLellan," she says with a smirk, retrieving her drone and offering a mock salute.

"At ease," are her last words, spoken lightly, teasingly, as she strides to the garage, long hair swaying, skirt ruffling in the cool breeze, her UAV held gently in her hands. Pilot follows close on her heels.

Is she flirting with me? "Later," I say lamely.

CHAPTER SEVEN

"*I MADE YOUR* favourite New York bagels for you," Mom says as I struggle to stuff the last few items into a giant canvas duffle bag Granddad has loaned me for the Outdoors Club camping trip. "Everyone will be jealous when you pull those out."

"Thanks, Mom." Way to help me fit in, *not*. I give her a quick hug and shove the wrapped onion bagels into my sack.

"Hope they don't make you homesick," she adds, leaning against the door frame of my bedroom, hands clasped. "They did me, just making them."

"They will if they're as good as the ones at Broadway Bagels." I humour her, referring to our favourite takeout back home. *No*, I correct myself, *not home anymore*. Even though I miss my friends like crazy, and miss lots of things about New York, my mother's over-the-top homesickness actually makes me want to try harder to like this place. Weird, but that's the way it is. Anyway, it's not like I had a girlfriend back there. And it would be wrong to move back while Granddad is ill. That's where I'm totally with Dad.

She sighs and strolls over to help me cram a pair of newly purchased wool socks into the overflowing bag. Her wedding ring catches on the bag, and her bracelets jangle as she struggles to pull it free.

"If I go back to New York for a visit in a few weeks, would you like to come with me?" She's twisting her ring with her fingers now.

I straighten up and study my fit, fashionably dressed mother, whose heavily made-up eyes won't quite meet mine. "In a few weeks? We only just got here, and I'm in school, Mom."

She lifts a manicured fingernail to her mouth and chews on it for a second. "You're right, Ray, of course. I just thought … Well, be careful on this trip, Ray. It's awfully cold and I know you hate camping, and I worry about …"

She walks over and smothers me in a hug, almost like she's clinging to me. Is her face slightly damp on my neck? I give her a dutiful squeeze back. "Got to close this duffle somehow," I mumble, trying to pull the drawstring tight. "Do you think I'm taking too much?"

"Ask your granddad," she suggests, pulling back and peering at me, her mascara slightly smudged.

"No way," I say, and we both laugh.

* * *

"Are you serious?" Vice-President Cole greets me when Mom discharges me in the school parking lot beside the lineup of Outdoors Club members and the waiting minibus. "You moving into the mountains for a month or something?"

Guess I brought too much. "Always prepared," I try to joke.

"As long as you're prepared to carry it," Mr. Mussett says, shaking his head.

"Min-jun here yet?" I ask, embarrassed. Great start.

"He'll be here," Cole says, glancing at his watch.

Dorothy appears and points to my duffle bag. "Brought your own log to sit on around the campfire?" A high-tech pink-and-purple pack hangs lightly off her shoulder. My face goes sunstroke hot.

"And marshmallows," I say. Crap. What kind of comeback is that?

She leans in, bringing with her a fruity scent of gum that makes me breathless. "Hope you didn't bring a drone," she says in a hushed voice, "or Mr. Mussett will chop you into fish bait."

"Then again, if disaster hits and we need a rescue, it might save the day," I reply, smiling.

I climb aboard the minibus and, because everyone else is sitting in chattering pairs, plunk down on a vinyl seat near the back. The second Dorothy sits down in front of me, Cole swings in beside her, though judging from her deep sigh, it isn't exactly by invitation. Club members continue to pile in, looking at the empty seat beside me like it has feces on it, no one saying a word to me. *I'm not disliked*, I tell myself. *Just temporarily untested.*

Finally, a pair of well-worn leather hiking boots stops beside my silver running shoes. "This taken?" asks a familiar voice. "Hope not, 'cause it's the last free seat."

"Min-jun! You made it!" I say with relief.

"Of course I made it. I'm president. By the way, your granddad said I need to keep an eye on you, but just so we're agreed, I'm not in the babysitting business."

"Affirmative," I say lightly, hoping Cole and Dorothy didn't hear him.

"No luck with the bear?" he asks as the driver starts up the bus.

I lower my voice. "The conservation officer says there was no sign of Hank and that he had full co-operation from the Logan brothers, who send their condolences for my loss." I roll my eyes.

"Yeah, right. Maybe your pet will wander into our camp this weekend," Min-jun jokes, elbowing me.

I push his elbow away. "I will find where they've put Hank, and I will rescue him," I say in a firm voice. And I will not indulge in darker thoughts about Hank's possible fate.

Min-jun shakes his head. "He hasn't been kidnapped, Ray, and that thing wouldn't survive a night in the wild on his own, even without a broken paw. Drop it, dude."

I feel a pain in my stomach, because I know he could be right. "Whatever," I say stiffly, as the bus pulls out onto the valley's only highway. "So, what's the plan?"

"Bus takes us up into the mountains, we walk in a few kilometres, set up our tents, and do campfire singalongs. Tomorrow we hike for eight hours and climb back on the bus."

"Eight hours?" I echo in horror.

"Kidding about the campfire singalongs and eight hours. What did you do for outings in New York City?"

"Took down muggers and ordered out for pizza."

He laughs, a big laugh for his compact body. But I'm well aware he's still trying to figure me out.

We jolt for half an hour on backroads that would take out the exhaust systems of most vehicles. My stomach goes as tight as a Yankees pitcher's grip. I pull off my beret and lower the window beside me as my gut contracts. Taking deep breaths, I try to picture something that's still — the Empire State Building in morning sunlight — to keep my stomach contents in place. But as the bus continues to jounce about, that bitter sensation crawls up my throat. Even as I clamp my mouth shut, I'm thinking, *Into the beret or out the window? Beret or window?*

"Hey, close that window! It's cold," Cole complains.

I half stand and vomit out the window and down the side of the bus. No way I'm going to spoil my favourite hat.

"Eeeew," chorus my busmates. Min-jun, Cole, and Dorothy all cover their faces and lean away from me.

"Sorry," I gasp.

"You can wash it when we get there," Cole grumbles.

When the bus finally shudders to a stop, I stagger off and use my water bottle and a spare T-shirt to clean up my mess. Shivering in the chilly May air, I stand beside a

sign with an arrow indicating the way to Forest Service
Campsite 78.

Memories of a long-ago early-spring camping trip
with Granddad and one of his hunting buddies make me
shiver as I hoist the rough canvas bag to my shoulder. My
left ear burns like a red-hot brand. That's something it
has done occasionally since "the event" happened when
I was five. Placing a cooling hand on it under my beret, I
start walking behind Min-jun and Cole, ignoring the get-
lost glare that Cole delivers. My face probably reflects the
white scattered clouds above. I turn once to stare at the
back of the retreating bus, using all my willpower not to
run after it as the woods seem to swallow us.

I can do this, I tell myself. Bear bells jingle on several
students' packs.

I watch Cole drop back to place himself beside
Dorothy, his face alight as he tries to draw her into conversation. She gives one-word answers, her face neutral,
and soon pulls back to giggle with girlfriends.

"Camped much?" Cole asks me, surging forward again
like he needs a target for his annoyance at being rebuffed.

I dodge his question. "With my granddad."

"And with an outdoors and bike club in New York City,"
he adds, studying me with a frown. His words sound
more like a challenge than confirmation of our first conversation at school. "What kind of bike do you ride?"

I should speak up right now, come clean: tell him
that I don't bike, camp, canoe, or walk more than I
have to. That I hate woods and dangerous animals and
snarky Outdoors Club members, and that I'm here only

because I can't live under the same roof as my granddad if I don't somehow get through this day.

"None at the moment, but I'm looking forward to this trip, and learning more about the area. Nice air up here."

"Nice air?" he says, mocking me. "Compared to what, a smoggy city?" He picks up speed and resumes his place at the head of the line, beside Min-jun.

"Your granddad is quite the famous outdoorsman in this valley," some guy behind me comments, as if to make up for Cole's rudeness.

"Yeah, I guess he is." If only outdoorsiness were genetic.

"Are those shoes for real?" He points to my silver running shoes, then moves away. What, fashion police even in the Outdoors Club?

Hey, I have Granddad's pack, his tent, and his send-off — "Don't get eaten by a bear or make too much a fool o' yerself." So what could go wrong? All I have to do is survive twenty-four hours of cold and misery to become a card-carrying member of the Outdoors Club. Extra credit if I impress Dorothy or avoid making a further fool of myself, both highly unlikely. I sigh and daydream of encountering Hank, who allows me to capture him and return him to the clinic.

Dorothy glides along the trail effortlessly, an orbit of chatty students — both male and female — hovering around her. She hasn't favoured me with so much as a glance since our earlier exchange. Waiting to see how I fit in. Which doesn't stop me from watching that long hair swing and wondering what it would feel like to run my hand through it. *Huh? Get real, Ray.*

Since no one's trotting near me and my attempts at starting conversations are getting me nowhere, I pull my binoculars out of my pack and pause occasionally to check out nearby tree branches and mountaintops, hoping to impress someone with a cool discovery — or to spot Hank. Fifteen minutes of on-and-off squinting later, I'm rewarded with a reddish dot catching the sun at the bottom of a nearby lush valley that runs down to an ocean inlet. Maybe it's a stop on our tour, an oceanfront hotel with hot chocolate and saunas? I picture sitting in a sauna beside Dorothy, and the chill air warms around me. But a closer look reveals the peeling red paint and glassless windows of a complex involving maybe twenty slumping buildings with holey roofs. They are covered in graffiti and surrounded by the remnants of paths filled with ferns and fallen trees. It's all beside a wooden pier held up by aging logs driven into the saltwater bay. My binoculars pick up a fisherman in a tiny camouflage motorboat drifting under the rotting dock.

"What're those ruins?" I ask the boy beside me.

He doesn't even bother looking through the binoculars. "An old cannery. Shut down ages ago."

So much for the sauna scenario. Huffing a little, I'm now at the very tail end of the line.

It feels like my bag has sheared off half my right shoulder by the time Mr. Mussett halts us in a clearing beside a small stream. "This is our camp, kids. Min-jun and Ray, you're on supper duty."

The flattest spot I can find is beside the stream at the near edge of the clearing, so I dump my stuff there and, with one eye on everyone else erecting their shelters, spill the contents out of the tent bag and try to fit the poles together like a 3-D puzzle. On the far side of the clearing, Min-jun puts his tent up in seconds. Cole, busy erecting his as close to Dorothy's as he can, is taking his time.

Long after the others have gathered around a crackling fire, Min-jun takes pity on me, points out that my tent pack is missing one pole, and helps me haul a sturdy stick from the forest floor that will finish the job.

"Your tent is almost an antique, bro. Your granddad's?"

"It's the same tent I camped in with him when I was five," I boast, then think to add, "He wouldn't let me use his nylon one."

"Sounds about right," he says, but I'm not sure I hear sympathy.

A giant pot of chili and foil-wrapped packages of cornbread are on the campfire by the time I arrive to help.

"You'll do dishes with Cole," Mr. Mussett says, raising one eyebrow.

After scooping some excellent-smelling chili into my tin bowl and chowing down on the cornbread while perched awkwardly on a fireside log, I decide things aren't so bad. We've done the worst bit, right? And although the woods are dark now, I'm surrounded by people, including an adult leader. When I catch Dorothy watching me, I nod, and I'm startled to get a high-wattage smile in return. Which earns me a glare from Cole.

"Most of you already know how to hang food bags from trees," Mr. Mussett is saying to the group, his eyes on me.

"Three metres above the ground, a metre from either tree. That's to keep bears from getting into them, of course."

I may hate the outdoors, but I probably know as much as this instructor, given how many vacations I've spent here over the years. Granddad and Dad were always sharing such info with me.

But I'm not about to say so when Mr. Mussett takes me aside and launches into a lecture on camping basics, from starting a fire to getting lost to avoiding or handling a bear encounter. "Stop and listen every five minutes or so," he instructs. "Talk if you're going around a blind bend. If you run into fresh tracks or scat, ripped-apart logs, or claw marks on trees, back away."

"How do you tell a grizzly track from a black bear track?" I ask, playing along.

"Grizzlies have long, straight claws, and black bears have shorter, curved ones," some smartass looking for a gold star responds.

"Exactly," Mr. Mussett confirms. "And if there's such a thing as a safe distance from a bear, it's seventy-five metres. That's the wingspan of a 747. Get any closer than that and it may feel threatened enough to charge."

I smile grimly and use all my energy to block memories of a certain incident in my past. I've heard that enough from Granddad over the years.

Mussett points out the different trees around us: Douglas fir ("the easiest to climb"), lodgepole pine, red cedar, hemlock, birch, and others. "Many of the fir and cedar trees are two hundred to five hundred years old. The Nuxalk people, as many of you know, have been here at least ten thousand years. They've traditionally used cedar for clothing, mats, baskets, canoes, totem poles, and planks for houses and boardwalks."

I see Dorothy smile proudly, and I raise an eyebrow as Mussett points to a red cedar with strips pulled off for these purposes. How cool is that? Definitely not the kind of thing Granddad ever pointed out.

"There are also trees rubbed smooth by bears deliberately leaving their scent behind for interested females," Mr. Mussett continues.

That gets a few giggles, but it starts my pulse pounding. No bear encounters here, please.

An hour or two after we've eaten supper and done the dishes, as we're still sitting on logs around the campfire, Cole asks me, "Singing campfire songs with us, new boy?"

"Thanks anyway," I reply, as I'm sure he hoped. Of course, no one starts singing songs. He was teasing.

"So what animal heads has your granddad mounted?" asks a freckled girl.

I smile appreciatively at this person who's actually trying to make me feel part of the group. After naming them off the best I can, I find myself engaged in chit-chat, including questions about the new vet clinic. No one asks about New York City. I guess for people here, it's as remote as the Amazon. But hey, some people are actually talking to me!

I mostly sit and listen, trying not to stare at Dorothy, who is cooking popcorn over the fire. She grants me the first helping and says, "Welcome to the club, new kid."

Though hoping to be promoted to *Ray* at some point, I nod and thank her. Half an hour later, when she says good night and leaves for her tent, Cole leans over and says in a low voice, "Don't even think about it, New York. She's mine."

"Mmm," I reply, yawning.

"Night everyone," Min-jun says, and I feel unexpectedly abandoned as he retreats to his orange pup tent in the far shadows. Time to traipse in the other direction and crawl into my leaning heap of worn canvas.

I'm running my headlamp batteries down by reading Granddad's wilderness survival manual when I hear Mr. Mussett say, "Time to turn in, everyone. Good night."

Poking my head out a little later, I note that a bunch of making-out couples have taken over the logs by the fire. Not including Dorothy, at least. I watch the sparks, hear the giggling and soft chatter, and ache for my friends and hangouts in New York City.

Arlo and I are teaching some kids droning on Saturday mornings, Koa wrote me recently. *We're earning good money. Don't know why the three of us never came up with the idea before. Could really use your help, tho! Get your butt back here? Nice pics of your new drone in progress. Will send you some of mine next time. Seriously, Ray, hope things are going okay for you out in the Canadian boonies.*

Halfway into the night, with my body chilled and my back as warped as a curly fry, I wriggle out, grab my can of bear spray and headlamp, and stumble away from camp to pee. So uncomfortable, camping! Then I decide to drag my tent a few feet to a flatter surface, which happens to be closer to the swollen stream. No longer sleepy, I walk around the quiet campsite to un-stiffen my legs, even though it's totally creepy among the trees at night.

Just as I'm about to head back to my shelter, I hear something big rustling in the trees at the far end of camp. Adrenalin shoots through me. A grizzly? I glance at the fire; neither a wisp of smoke nor a sign of linger-ing lovers remains. Listening carefully, I judge that the creature is bigger than a raccoon, but smaller than an adult grizzly. Maybe.

"Anyone there?" I whisper. It pauses. Insanely, I pic-ture Hank.

Clutching my bear spray, fighting my lifetime terror of the woods, I make my way toward the noise, wearing only my red brand-name boxers, unlaced silver shoes, and City That Never Sleeps hoodie.

I hear the snapping of cedar boughs and the crunch of twigs and pine needles just ahead in the forest. The creature is not stealthy enough to be a cougar, I'm guess-ing, and whatever it is, it's moving away from camp. A deer? Coyote? Apparently out of my mind, I follow it down a trail for perhaps ten minutes, half-terrified, half-determined, knowing I'm being totally, utterly stu-pid because there's no way it's Hank.

I'm ready to turn around when my beam picks it up: a ghostly white body almost floating through the woods, angling down a steepening trail.

CHAPTER EIGHT

A SCREAM IS strangled in my throat when the form turns and looks at me with unseeing eyes. "Min-jun," I whisper, half registering that he's sleepwalking in his white pyjamas. "Min-jun?"

He turns and ambles on like I'm not there, accelerating his pace on the uneven ground. It seems as if he's headed for the bottom of the deep valley I saw earlier.

I should lunge forward, tap him on the shoulder, and wake him before he trips headfirst into a ravine or some dangerous animal jumps us. Instead, I keep following him like a mesmerized sleepwalker myself. Normally I'm scared at even the notion of being in the woods at night, but following the Outdoors Club leader puts a strange calm in me. I tell myself if anything happens, he'll wake up instantly and handle it for me. Anyway, what harm is there in putting one foot in front of another after him, for just a few more yards, 'cause I'm curious to see where he's going?

Ten minutes later, where the trail begins to switchback more steeply downwards, he pauses in front of a barbed-wire fence and stares across it into the darkness. I stand a few feet behind, hoping he's not going to try going under it, since it obviously marks private property. Finally, I open my mouth to shout at him. That's when he lifts his head and stares intently above us, like he has heard something. He raises an arm slowly, rotating his head and body while pointing a finger, like he's signalling a galactic starship.

I look up at the incredibly clear array of stars, nothing like you'd see from a city. I identify the Big Dipper, which I remember is part of Ursa Major: Great Bear. How appropriate, here in the Great Bear Rainforest. Then I notice tiny white dots that don't look like they fit in. Falling stars? A soundless airplane with lit-up windows? I switch off my headlamp and stand as still as my sleepwalker friend. Then I hear it too: the buzz of a hummingbird. But hummingbirds don't fly at night. Hardly any birds do, Dad told me once. Only owls and nighthawks. And the object is flying way too high to be a bird. Wait! I know that sound! It's a drone! A stealth drone with low-noise propellers, hovering high over-head, observing us. I'd never have heard it if Min-jun hadn't looked up and pointed. How did he hear it?

Squinting into the night sky, I hardly breathe as it lowers, very slowly, until it's something like ten stories over us, an otherworldly UFO. It's a big-money, super-high-tech drone. The kind only a government spy agency or criminal gang might have. A red light on its sensor flashes rapidly like someone is taking pictures.

Is this seriously happening?

A crunch close at hand breaks the spell. It's Min-jun sprinting off-trail, stumbling in a panic, crashing through brush.

The drone's camera flicks out and it floats up and away quietly, as if it were never there. Or maybe like it just realized we might've spotted it? I watch the dark form skitter away like a giant bat against a universe of luminous dots, headed at breathtaking speed for the depths of the valley in front of us, or the bay beyond.

A scream jerks my head around, and I leap off the trail and switch on my headlamp.

"Min-jun!" I shout and I step off trail with arms in front to ward off branches, shivering now in my boxers, shoes, and hoodie. I hear splashing and more scream-ing. He must have reached the stream and tripped in! It's too shallow to pose a danger, but cold enough to chill someone who's plopped in it. My fault! Why didn't I nab him earlier? I sprint, ignoring thorns and salal leaves whiplashing my calves. I wade in and grab his hands as he sits hip deep in the running water.

I brace myself against a boulder and pull till he's on the bank. Then I put my face in his. "I've got you, Min-jun. You're okay. You were sleepwalking."

But his eyes are still black hollows, and his bluish lips are smacking, smacking, smacking. His teeth clamp down on his tongue till it bleeds, and his hands jerk from side to side, like he's trying to swim.

My mind flashes back to an afternoon in my parents' New York City clinic when a French bulldog with a white studded collar had an epileptic seizure. I know instantly now what to do. I roll Min-jun onto his side to prevent fluids from getting into his lungs and make sure his tongue isn't blocking his airway. Then I launch myself on top of him to keep him from hurting himself and to warm him as much as I can. Though his teeth continue gnashing, I remember not to insert a stick or finger, which can cause vomiting and make things worse. Episodes are over quickly, right? Is it the same for humans as for dogs? I wish my parents and their vet cabinet were here.

Where are Mr. Mussett, the late-night couples, and the mystery drone when we need them?

Min-jun calms within minutes, as I hoped he would. But he's groggy and a little incoherent — if he's like the bulldog he will be for about half an hour. I peel off his wet pyjama top and remove my warm sweatshirt to put it on him. His dripping bottoms will have to stay on till we get back to his tent. Ignoring the squish of water in my favourite shoes, I pull, push, tug, and coax Min-jun uphill back to the trail. Helping him is all that keeps me from freaking out in this darkness. What was I thinking, following him? But good thing I did. He pauses as we step back onto the trail, obviously disoriented.

"Easy, Min-jun. We're going back to camp now. You've had a seizure. A grand mal." His eyes focus on me and he seems to register me clearly for the first time.

"Don't — tell — anyone — I have seizures. Please, Ray. Or I'll — make — life — hell for you."

Huh?

His lids flutter closed again.

"Min-jun, we have to get back to your tent. I won't tell anyone, okay? Just move before you get hypothermia or something."

"Uh-huh." He leans into me heavily and lurches up the trail beside me.

"And please answer two questions. Are you on medication for seizures, and how often do you have them?"

"I take something," he says tiredly. "I've had seizures once every few months all my life. Don't tell —"

"Chill. I won't. I promised."

He just needs to sleep it off, I decide. But he's definitely starting to shiver from his cold dip. I must get him back before he gets dangerously chilled. I don't know how to treat hypothermia without looking at my granddad's manual back in my tent.

We manage to reach his tent without running into further stealth flyers, though I switch off my headlamp when I hear people talking at the other end of camp.

Dawn sends its first streaks of grey light skittering across the sky as I roll Min-jun into his tent, towel him down, throw his wet clothes into a corner, and zip him into his sleeping bag. He falls asleep instantly. I turn him onto his side and check his breathing, then, with my damp sweatshirt in one hand, I poke my head out of his tent, praying no one has seen us.

I see bare feet in front of my face. Feet with polished toenails. How do I know they're Dorothy's even before I lift my head?

She has a finger over her lips. "They're out searching for you," she whispers. "Was Min-jun walking in his
sleep?"

I nod.

"He did that once before. I woke him up, steered him
back to his tent, and never told anyone. Didn't want to
embarrass him."

"Oh." Then it occurs to me: "Were you flying a drone
just now, Dorothy?"

"What? A drone? Of course not. It's dark, in case you
hadn't noticed. And I'm not interested in getting kicked
out of the club for bringing one on this trip. Why? Is
that what you were doing?" She flips her mane of hair
as she stands there in fleece long underwear, a sleeping
bag like a shawl over her shoulders and an accusing look
on her face.

"When I followed Min-jun, there was a huge stealth
drone with a thermal camera and low-noise propellers
flying more than two hundred feet above us."

Even in the early-morning shadows, I register her
frown before she whips her head toward the valley for
a second. A hand rises to her chest, then curls tightly
and drops to her side. She shakes her head, not looking
at me.

"You're nuts," she whispers. "Imagining things. It's
five o'clock in the morning and Cole and Mussett are
out looking for you. Get your ass back to your tent, idiot."

She melts into the shadows and I sprint across camp
to the other side. Only to slam into Mr. Mussett.

"And where have *you* been, McLellan?"

"Um, I was answering the call of nature and stretching my legs when I accidentally walked into the stream," I say, wishing I could tell the whole truth so he would call 911 and clap me on the back for saving the club's president. *But I promised.*

"Cole noticed your tent tilted over and getting wet by the edge of the stream. It seems you didn't anchor it well, and you thought it made sense to move it *almost into the stream*? Cole was concerned and woke me half an hour ago to report you weren't in it."

I glance uneasily toward my tent and wonder whether I've really been missing that long. Mussett says nothing about Min-jun, so I assume no one but Dorothy knows a second person was missing, too.

"Hey, everyone!" Cole shouts, making me jump. A few students poke sleepy heads out of their tents, some with flashlights in their hands. "This seems to be as good a time as any to discuss the right time of day to hike, and whether it's safe to hike alone. As in, the new kid just returned from a half-hour solo night trek. During bear-mating season, I might add."

"Cole," Mussett says, clearly annoyed.

I stand there in my red boxers and silver shoes, holding my damp hoodie, shivering in their flashlight beams and wondering, *Which light is Dorothy's?*

Sniggers.

I bite my tongue and pull on my hoodie.

"But since I can see you're actually *underdressed* for the occasion for once, city boy" — chuckles and giggles from our groggy audience as Cole continues —

"let's restrict our discussion to the treatment for hypothermia, which you might have contracted if you hadn't found your way back after apparently wading into the stream."

"Campers," Mussett orders, "go back to sleep. Cole, I don't think this is necessary."

A male voice speaks up. "Strip him and put him in a sleeping bag with a naked girl. Any volunteers?"

Giggles.

"Or?" Cole prompts, aiming his flashlight at Dorothy, who stands hunched, staring at the ground, her sleeping bag having fallen to her slim waist.

She looks up, unsmiling, her gaze trained on Mr. Mussett rather than on Cole or me. "Give him a hot drink and let him go back to his tent," she says. "And let the rest of us go back to sleep, too."

"Exactly," our teacher says.

"But!" Cole says, his voice raised. "One more point. Do we pitch tents close to a stream in early spring, when melting ice farther up the mountain is swelling that stream?" He's looking at me, but I sense that answering would not score me any points.

The kids turn their heads toward my tent, helpfully illuminated by Cole's extra-strong beam. The slump of canvas sits with one corner in the tumbling water. At least it hasn't been carried downstream.

"Noooo," chorus my fellow students, some of them yawning.

"Give him a break," Dorothy says through gritted teeth, which warms me slightly.

"Back to sleep till sun-up, then," Mr. Mussett says. "Enough, Cole. And good night, Ray."

I catch Cole's head turning from Dorothy to me as I stumble toward the stream bed. I unstake my heavy, old-school tent and drag it back to its first position. Then I burrow into my damp sleeping bag and close my eyes.

Ten minutes later, in the stillness, I get up again and tiptoe over to check on Min-jun: fast asleep, breathing evenly, and cozy warm. So I go back to my own digs, though I'm destined not to sleep another minute of the night. Of course, no one offers me a hot drink as I lie awake contemplating night-vision drones — and dreaming of completing my own.

CHAPTER NINE

"*DISGRACED YERSELF AND* yer family name!" Granddad blasts me. He's propped in his chair by the wood stove with a blanket up to his chin. "Tent minus a pole and pitched half in a stream, midnight hiking in yer skivvies —"

I stand in front of him like a condemned prisoner. It's not the time, if there ever is one, to claim Min-jun was sleepwalking or ask about our neighbour's condition — and who's going to believe a story about a lit-up drone come to visit us in the night?

"Ray's back safely. That's all that matters," Dad says.

"Stupid as a brick," Granddad mumbles.

"How dare you!" Mom says.

"Honey —" Dad places a hand on Mom's shoulder.

She brushes it off like a poisonous spider has landed there. "Well, I'm taking him out to celebrate his return.

It'll be a mom-and-son dinner. You two can fix whatever you find here," she says icily, grabbing my hand and her purse and marching me toward the door.

I look to Dad, waiting for him to defend us, join us, or stop us. But he just shakes his head and slumps into a chair, looking as defeated as a benched player.

"Was it pretty up there, at least?" Mom asks at the diner, smiling warmly, her hands cupping the striped mug of tea a waitress has handed her. She's wearing lots of lipstick, like she's on a date rather than running away from home with her son to a place that has all of five vinyl booths.

"I guess. No sign of Hank," I say.

She shakes her head. "Son, if you're going to be a vet, you have to learn to let go of animals that don't make it. It's a reality of our profession."

I clench my jaw and pretend to scan the plasticized menu.

"Scrambled eggs and bacon," I tell the waitress, since there's no eggs Benedict or matzo ball soup, my favourites back home. Er, in the city. Thinking of the city makes me feel homesick, makes me want to reach for my phone to text Arlo and Koa.

"Their Manhattan steak and New York fries aren't bad, considering where we are," Mom says with a twinkle in her eye, like we're sharing an inside joke. "Bet you miss your Coney Island hot dogs."

I glance sideways at the grey-haired waitress, who's pretending she hasn't heard.

"No," I say truthfully.

"I'll take the steak and fries," Mom orders, and the waitress nods and moves away.

"Mom, epilepsy is when someone ... er, dogs ... have seizures, right? What causes that?"

She smiles and takes my hand across the red Formica table, always proud when I ask her vet questions. "Both people and animals can be born with epilepsy. It's just abnormal signalling in the brain. Or it can start due to a brain injury or liver failure. Epileptic seizures are actually the most common brain disorder in dogs. And seizures are often preceded by something called an aura — where the dog is hyperalert, almost psychic, in its sight, smell, and sound. The seizures are typically triggered by stressful phenomena, such as blinking lights."

"Oh," I say, remembering Min-jun's startling ability to hear the drone before I did and his collapse after it went into blinking mode. That's *if* there really was a drone, and we weren't *both* sleepwalking.

"An epileptic seizure involves a jerking activity in a specific muscle group that can spread, and sometimes the victim bites its tongue, but it's important never to —"

"— insert anything into its mouth unless its tongue is blocking its airway. I remember."

"Good, Ray. Epilepsy is easily controlled with medication, and hardly anyone dies of it, though they can sometimes break a limb thrashing about. What's important is to prescribe the right medication and watch for any increase in frequency, which can lead to stasis, which is —"

"— a seizure someone doesn't come out of. Can die from."

"Exactly."

I nod and make room on the table for the huge orange plates that hold large portions of steaming food. Mom lights into her steak like she hasn't eaten for a while. Then her fork pauses.

"Why, Ray? A friend's dog has epilepsy?"

She thinks I have a friend. I should have by now, of course. Never mind that Min-jun avoided me in a weird, nervous way the rest of the trip. Like he was embarrassed about what went down. But according to my reading on epilepsy since then, he probably doesn't remember everything. And then there was Dorothy, who would thoughtfully drop back on the trail to encourage me when I lagged, which definitely put a spring in my step. Not that that makes her my *friend*. And it certainly didn't win me points with Cole.

"Earth to Ray." Mom is waving a fry in my face, her brow wrinkled.

"No, no friend with an epileptic dog. Just studying the clinic's manuals," I lie. Why am I lying to my own mother? Why not tell her about Min-jun, get her to ask Mr. Kim whether his son's on medication? Does the school or Outdoors Club even know he has seizures? It seems risky for them not to know. *But I promised.*

"Epilepsy." Mom sighs. "You know, there's such a stigma against it that some people won't ask for help. Centuries ago, people blamed it on evil spirits, and tossed people who suffered from it in with lepers. But it's a simple physical ailment, and controllable in eighty percent of cases. Dogs with seizures? That's something you need to know about if you're going to be a vet." She pats my shoulder like I'm a dog, then cocks her head to look at me more closely.

I wonder if the Kims feel a stigma about Min-jun's epilepsy.

"You're not very happy here, are you, Ray?"

No! I want to say. I want Arlo and Koa, and I want my Central Park droning fun, and my old high school and food haunts and subways and noise. But I don't want it to be Mom and me against Dad and Granddad.

"I'm trying," I say. It's true, and life would be easier if she would try, too.

She sighs. "I've told Sean we should hire a caregiver for his father and get out of here. I'm sorry your granddad is ill, but it might be months before … I don't see why …"

My mind wanders to what Dad recently told me about Granddad's father, that he was a penniless immigrant who left Ireland to live in Canada's western wilderness. "He was tough as leather," Dad said, "and the family lived hand to mouth. If Granddad is stubborn and a skilled outdoorsman, it's because that's what he and his older brothers had to be to stay alive. I hurt him a lot by settling in a city so far away. But I'll make it up to him these final months, as best I can."

I study my eggs and refuse to look at Mom.

"I think we'll be moving back soon, Ray." Her eyes dance a little when I look up. "Good thing we only leased our clinic and sublet our apartment in New York, just in case this didn't work out."

"Dad would leave Granddad?" I blurt out.

Her long lashes blink as she surveys me like she has only just realized I'm in the same booth. "We've left him at the end of every vacation we've ever had here," she says in a measured tone. "Including the one where you lost your ear."

I reach up and pull my beret lower, then stab at my eggs.

"What exactly do you remember about that trip, Ray?"

The eggs feel rubbery in my mouth now, and my pulse races, like it always does when she gets on this topic. "I was five, Mom. I don't remember anything."

Though I fight against it, an image comes to me of waking up in a tent all alone, shivering. Terrified. I hear shuffling outside by the campfire, but no voices. Granddad and his friend are supposed to be out there, chatting, keeping the fire strong, protecting me till they crawl in for the night.

I stick my head out of the tent, but then everything goes white, like the film of my memory is burning up from the edges inward. The film frames flicker and snap, revealing nothing till I'm in a bed at Bella Coola Hospital. The bandaged side of my head is throbbing and a doctor is hovering over me. Mom hugs and rocks me with tears running down her face as Dad stands beside us in his quiet, caring way. It hurts, but whatever happened is over. Everything's okay. Except that the whole thing was —

"It was my fault," I say in a dull voice. I've said it so many times, despite my unclear memories. It's the only thing I'm certain of. "It was my fault."

"But —"

"Stop it!" I say it louder than I mean to. The waitress pauses in the middle of taking another table's order and the short-order cook looks at us through the pass-through window from the steamy kitchen. Mom pushes her back erect against the booth seat, her red lips forming a surprised *oh*.

With effort, I lower my voice. "I was only five. I don't remember."

"Exactly. You were only five. How could you remember?"

There's silence for a moment.

"He has never accepted me, you know," she says with bitterness. "I do so much for him, and he never even says thank you. And the ear incident —"

My left ear is burning now, here in the diner, the pain building. There's the pounding, like a train is driving through my head. There's agony and terror. I want to cover my ear with one hand, want to push the fingers of my other hand into the water glass in front of me, take out some ice cubes, and press them against the wound. Instead, I lock my fingers together in my lap and let the heat continue to sear the side of my head, enter my skull, veer, and shoot out through my eyes, like flaming arrows aimed at my mother.

"He's dying, Mom. Leave it," I growl. I have spoken to her like this a few times before, but never so vehemently.

She raises her paper napkin to dab at her lips.

"I'm finished," she says calmly, folding her napkin into four parts like it's a linen one at a Ritz-Carlton luncheon. She is speaking in her totally-under-control vet voice, the one that reduces stress levels at the Bella Coola clinic each day and allows us to proceed with whatever emergency bursts through the doors. Dog crises, that's what my parents do well. But the barking and clawing that have been increasing between her and Dad and Granddad? That's another story.

"Let's go home," I say, and for a split second, her lit-up face tells me she has misunderstood. We seem to have different definitions of *home*.

CHAPTER TEN

"HEY, ARLO! Are you growing a moustache or am I seeing things? No way!"

We're on Skype, sharing news and enjoying seeing one another's faces.

"Yes way," he says. "You're just jealous, I know. Hey, is that your bedroom? Looks like a log cabin. Are you seriously living in a log cabin, Rayster?"

"With the heads of animals hung all around us in the living room," I inform him. "My granddad's a taxidermist, I told you!"

"Too weird," Koa says, poking his head onto the screen in front of Arlo. "So, you said you've almost got a fleet of three? And what was all this about a drone chick? Maybe this Bella Coola place is all right after all!"

I laugh. "Yup, I have them lined up right here on my bed. I'm going to introduce you to them one at a time!"

I line up Bug, Butterfly, and Skyliner and fill my friends in on all the technical challenges and accomplishments associated with them. They cheer when I tell them Skyliner is going to be waterproof with thermal capabilities, and they *ooh* and *ahh* over him when I turn him around slowly for the screen, like a prizewinning show dog.

"Ray, are you doing your homework like you promised?" comes my mom's voice from the clinic. Uh-oh.

"Guys, my mom's on the prowl. Gotta go for now. Talk to you next week?"

"Sure, and bring this drone chick on-screen then, Rayster!" Arlo teases.

Quickly I sign off, then shuffle outside and lie down in the hammock beside my laptop and schoolbooks, even though a greying sky threatens to let loose a rainstorm.

"Yes, Mom, doing my homework."

I actually work on an assignment for a few minutes. But it starts to sprinkle, and here in this sling, my mind soon flits to Hank. I'm wishing he would appear, push his nose into me, and spring into my lap. Where is he? Is he still alive? Is someone feeding him? Poachers don't kill the younger ones. Who really took him and why?

I move under cover of the porch and my fingers tap out questions for the all-knowing Google. "Where's Hank?" That takes me to an eatery three thousand miles away. "Why steal a bear?" A news report details a toy-store robbery of giant teddy bears. Other questions produce info on gummy bears, the Chicago Bears, bears featured in an online game, and economic predictions based on bear versus bull markets. Markets! That's it!

"Who sells real bears?" I type on the keyboard. And then, recalling the right word, "Why *poach* a bear?"

My deck chair vibrates as I sit up straight and stare at the screen. "No way!"

"No way what?" It's Min-jun's voice. He's coming out our back door with a tray and an empty mug. "Just delivered my dad's special healing tea to your grandfather," he says, and pauses as awkwardness hangs between us. "I owe you an apology, dude. Dorothy told me I walked in my sleep the other night and you rescued me. I thought I might have, but wasn't sure. I don't always remember. She said you took a lot of crap for not telling anyone."

"Something like that," I say hesitantly.

He sets the tray down and pulls a nearby stool up beside me to peek at my screen. "Whatcha got there, neighbour?"

I look at him curiously. So he barely remembers the sleepwalking, and no longer recalls the epileptic seizure at all. Not unusual, I guess, based on what I've read.

"Stare much?" he teases as I continue to study his face.

"Sorry. I just asked Doctor Google why anyone would want a young bear from the wild, and look what it told me."

Min-jun groans. "You're not still obsessing about that cub being stolen, Ray. Forget the little guy. You hardly knew it." But he peers at my screen and reads aloud. "A bear's gallbladder is worth three thousand bucks in parts of Asia? They're sold in velvet-lined boxes? You can buy bear skulls, hide, and claws online? That's gross, bro."

"A bowl of bear-claw soup costs a thousand dollars," I read aloud with bitterness. "Bear parts are a two-billion-dollar industry worldwide. And bear bile is worth more per ounce than heroin. It's found in the gallbladder."

"What's bear bile? Where is a gallbladder?" Min-jun asks, wrinkling his nose.

I jab a finger at my lower chest. "Bile is a fluid made by the liver and then stored in the gallbladder. It helps break down food." I'm quoting Mom, but, being a nice guy, I spare him the bit about bile being part of vomit.

"What, you're a vet already?"

"Affirmative," I kid back, then read on from the internet. "Some people believe bear gallbladders cure almost anything. They're found in shops that sell traditional medicine. Lots of countries are clamping down and trying to educate the public and prevent poached bear parts being sold on the black market." Then I add what my mom told me. "There are herbs and synthetic biles that do the same thing people believe bear bile does."

"And what's this got to do with anything?" he asks impatiently. He leans back on his stool and eyes the tray he's supposed to deliver back home, through what is now a downpour.

"Granddad says there are poachers around here. And we saw the Logans' Plott hounds, a breed used to hunt down bears. I've been asking around, and evidently the Logans don't farm anything up on their property anymore. I mean, like cows or wheat or stuff. So what are they living on?"

"Um, welfare, like lots of other people? You've added two and two together and gotten five," Min-jun says.

"If they've got Hank, they're in deep trouble with me," I say, "especially if they're treating animals badly for profit. I'll follow them, spy on them, trespass up there on their property, if that's what it takes." And they'd better not have killed him!

"Dude, you're seriously worked up. You're scaring me."

I wrinkle my face and do an imitation of Granddad's peevish voice: "A bear stripped o' his skin, paws, and gallbladder and left on the mountainsides for the vultures looks eerily like a man."

"Oh my god," Min-jun says, "you are so *him* when you do that. Promise me you won't really be him when you get old? 'Cause we'll probably still be neighbours, me coming over to bring you tea and pull your blanket up."

I laugh. "Your dad is good to my granddad. I hear he's taking him out to dinner tonight. Korean food, of course." I scroll down the screen, read some more, and feel all humour evaporate. "Min-jun, have you heard of bear-bile farms?"

"No."

"Where they milk caged bears."

"Milk 'em?" His expression is disbelieving.

"Says here instead of killing young bears and cutting out their gallbladders, they cage them, push a tube into their gut, and collect the gallbladder drippings, which they turn into pills and stuff."

"Sold in velvet boxes." His voice has gone flat.

"It's extremely painful for the bears," I read. "They mostly die of infections from the puncture hole, or from liver cancer. Grizzlies live fifteen to twenty-five years in the wild, but only a third of that if they're caged for bile collection."

He's staring at Hank's aged scat on the lawn, now disintegrating in the rain. "Dude, stop making yourself crazy. Maybe Hank just crossed the road and found a stepmom and is living happily ever after. Anyway, we saw inside the Logans' barn. There weren't any bears in there, let alone ones being milked. Just dogs."

"And dog *cages* that could fit young bears."

Min-jun shakes his head. "Not taking you up there again, bro. And those guys aren't going to listen to a dental hygiene speech next time. My advice?" He points to my discarded schoolbooks. "Get back to your homework. You can do mine when you're done with yours."

He scoops up his tray, and hurries home through the rain. All seven paces between our properties.

"Ray!" It's Dad's voice.

"Ray!" Mom's echoes from the clinic.

I lay my laptop and books aside and dash in, hoping for an interesting case, but halt when I see a cream-coloured miniature poodle with a pink collar standing unsteadily on the operating table, whimpering pitifully, with blood-stained white gauze sticking to her belly. I raise my eyes to meet the pale face of the client: Dorothy.

"She got bitten in a fight with another dog," she says in a small voice, eyeing all three of us in turn. "She came in bleeding and staggering. We tried to treat her ourselves but it looks bad. Can you do something? Will she be okay?"

"Ray, do you want to comment before we offer our diagnosis and take action?" my mother asks. Dorothy looks from Mom to me.

I turn to don a lab coat, scrub my hands at the sink, and pull on rubber gloves. Then I place my hands gently on Pilot's small pink belly: "It's a puncture wound. Maybe septic already."

"Correct, but that doesn't cover everything. Notice how she's shaking her head?" Mom says.

"And scratching her ears," Dad prompts, giving me an encouraging look.

I inspect the poodle's ears. "So, besides the BDLD wound, she has spear grass in her ear and it has caused an infection."

I've always loved the BDLD acronym, which stands for *big dog/little dog*. And spear grass is simply a long blade of grass that has pierced the tender inside of the ear. Dorothy is stroking her dog's neck with a shaking hand. A tear spills from her brimming chestnut eyes. I want to catch it with a finger and draw her into my arms.

Instead, I say, "She needs an otoscope exam right away. We'll remove the spear grass and treat her ear infection with antibiotic ointment. She needs antibiotics for the infected wound, too. Dorothy, do you want to come back in an hour, or stay?"

"I'll stay," she says, lifting her chin.

"Are you okay with Ray assisting with the treatment under our supervision?" Dad asks. "He has done these procedures before as part of his training."

"Of course!" Dorothy says. She gives me a look through her wet eyelashes that prompts me to grow a foot taller.

Mom takes the particulars with a clipboard while Dad administers a sedative. I shave around the poodle's belly wound, disinfect the area with antibacterial soap, place a drain, and suture the puncture, all under the watchful eyes of my parents, who occasionally hold out instruments like they're surgical nurses.

"Take a break, son," Mom says when it's finished. "I'll deal with the spear grass."

"Yes, excellent job. You've earned a rest," Dad says in his quiet voice, standing beside Mom like they're a tight, happy team. For this microsecond.

"She should come to in around thirty minutes, but she'll be sleepy for a while after that," I inform Dorothy as I remove my lab coat and hang it on a hook. I strip off my gloves, wash my hands, and don my beret and scarf, then shuffle outside after her. Together on the front porch, we watch the rain beat down.

"Thanks," she says in a low voice, her fingertips almost brushing mine. "You're okay, you know. You should wear that."

"Wear what? Why is everyone so hung up on what I wear?"

She giggles and I look at her quizzically. "You should 'wear' the fact that you're okay. Look proud and confident at school or on camping trips, like you do in your clinic and like you did when you were helping Min-jun after he sleepwalked. Wear who you really are, instead of walking around hunched like someone's going to hit you, or like you don't deserve a friend."

"I'm that bad, huh? Do I deserve *you* as a friend?" Bravely, I take her hand.

Instead of pulling it out of my grip, she interlaces her fingers in mine, tosses her hair, and gives me a smile that makes me want to sing at Carnegie Hall.

"How's the drone?" she asks.

"Butterfly is doing all right. I just need to figure out why her batteries aren't lasting longer. I'm not sure what else to do at this point. I've tried all kinds of batteries."

"What if I told you I build my own batteries?"

"Seriously? That's incredible. How'd you —?"

"It's a secret. Proprietary." She nudges my shoulder and giggles. "And you're wanting better batteries for what reason? To duel with me again? To film Bella Coola's scenery, because you're starting to like this place?"

"To duel, but not necessarily with you," I joke.

"I see," she says, eyes going dark for a split second. She looks toward the road and suddenly extracts her hand from mine.

Stopped on his bike in front of the house is Cole Thompson.

"New York, New York," Cole says in a raw tone. "How is Disarray Ray? Shouldn't you be studying your grandfather's soggy survival manual to prepare for your next outdoor adventure?"

So he searched my tent that night while I was down-slope dealing with Min-jun.

"Nope, I'm good, thanks to your excellent tutoring," I reply. "What do you say we get permission to fly drones on the next camping trip? Dorothy and I could show people how to fly them, and talk about how they can save lives in the wilderness."

"Ray McLellan can pronounce the word *wilderness*," Cole muses. "But we have other ways of saving lives here, new boy. And remote-control toys don't fall under woodsmanship." He glances as Dorothy. "Or woods-womanship," he allows, tipping his baseball cap with a nod and grimace. "See you around." And he speeds down the road with more calf-muscle action on display than necessary, rear tire spattering mud up his backside.

"If Mussett would give us permission, that would be cool," says my drone chick. "But it'll never happen."

"Then let's do our own drone flights," I suggest. "Know a good place without trees or people around?"

She looks thoughtful for a moment. "Yeah, there's a new clear-cut along a bay not far from here by boat."

"Granddad has a canoe. Can you paddle?" I've paddled his old aluminum canoe before, of course: each and every vacation here, with Granddad always hollering at me to pull harder. Or with Dad, on more peaceful outings.

"Of course I can paddle!" she says, rolling her eyes. "It's maybe forty minutes by canoe."

"Perfect," I say, not knowing if I can actually pull on a paddle for an entire forty minutes. "Maybe I can get the Jeep off Granddad to drive to the launch."

She shrugs. "I'm in. But when are you going to show me your UAV workshop? We have a few minutes before Pilot comes out of it, right?"

"We do." As we walk through the house to the backyard, I picture the two of us alone together in my workshop, her eyes alighting on my treasures and registering my mastery of the craft. Her excitement extending to a hug, which could turn into a —

"Ray?"

"Yes?"

"Is that your workshop?"

She's pointing to the right place, but half my workshop's contents are lying on the ground outside, along with the door's padlock, which has been sliced through by a buzz saw or some such.

"What?" I scream, and break into a sprint. As I enter the structure, Dorothy on my heels, I see Granddad's portion of the space untouched. This was a targeted attack. My drone parts are scattered and broken, some of my tools are missing, the overhead light bulb in my workspace is smashed, and shelves are hanging off the wall. Like a gorilla with a tire iron and a migraine headache has been around.

I take a deep breath to control a sharp surge of anger. Then, with a wave of relief, I remember: My three drones are safely in my bedroom, on my bed, still posed for photos to send to Arlo and Koa.

CHAPTER ELEVEN

MR. KIM IS the first to appear, holding an umbrella over his head, as Dorothy and I stand on the back patio out of the rain, staring at the workshop.

"You bang in workshop? Sound angry," he scolds, waving his free arm. He's dressed in jeans with an ironed crease and a new sweater, clearly making an effort to cheer up Granddad on their night out to his café. The way I'm feeling, I'm surprised I even register that.

"It's been vandalized," I cry out. "Did you see anyone? A bike? A truck? A person?" I swing around, looking everywhere.

Dorothy has her hands to her face and is shaking her head. "This doesn't happen in Bella Coola."

Mr. Kim looks from me to the workshop. "I see no one. Thought you work more noisy than usual. Min-jun!" he shouts.

My neighbour gallops out. "What's going on?" He looks at the mess, then at Dorothy, his dad, and me.

"Vandalized," I say. "Did you hear or see anything, Min-jun?"

He shakes his head slowly. "I heard noise, but thought it was you. Don't remember hearing a vehicle."

I call out for Mom and Dad, and while Dorothy explains the situation to them, Min-jun, Mr. Kim, and I check the alley and yard, but come up with no fresh vehicle tracks. Unfortunately, any footprints on the soggy ground are now destroyed by our own.

Pretty soon Granddad is tottering around the workshop, checking his own valuables and shaking his head at my room. He voices some of my own questions. "What eejit would come looking to steal in here? Looks to me like they had a mission concerning drones. You been spying on anyone, grandson? Have an enemy already? Or are yer parts worth more than I thought? Seems dangerous to share quarters with you, I'm thinking. Jae-bum and I will contemplate it more over dinner, will we Jae? Meantime, Ray, I suggest you clean up and slap another lock on it quick smart."

Mom speaks up. "What about calling the police before we touch anything?"

"For a few tools and toy parts?" Granddad bellows. "In Bella Coola, we let our law enforcement stay focused on real crimes. Right, Sean?"

Dad shrugs. "I need to check on the poodle," he says, ducking back into the clinic.

"I'll come with you," Dorothy says, giving me a sympathetic look before trailing after my dad.

I want to pound my fists on Granddad's disappearing back as he and Mr. Kim head to Mr. Kim's car. But evidently his monthly night out is more important than a break-in that involves only my belongings.

Who did this? Cole? The Logan brothers? A random thief who prefers drone tools to taxidermy tools? Or *have* I earned an enemy already?

The next weekend our paddles dip rhythmically into the calm waters of the bay, with me in the stern struggling to keep the canoe straight and Dorothy in the bow, powering us with the confidence of a girl who grew up here. She's wearing a pink fleece jacket, she's humming, and her black hair is flying free in the spring breeze.

Eagles pip-pip above us and we glide past the trees on shore, heading for the secluded inlet. Our cooler of picnic goodies is stashed in the canoe's centre, and our drones are lashed on top of it. My body is tingling with excitement for this drone date.

"Your dad doesn't mind us canoeing around the inlet?" I ask her.

A chuckle comes from the front. "He thinks I'm at the library studying."

"Oh."

"Nice of your granddad to loan you his Jeep and canoe."

"Anything to make me into a Bella Coolan outdoorsman," I say. "Or get rid of me for a few hours."

She laughs lightly.

"So this place we're going is good for flying drones?" I ask.

"It's Forest Service land that some lumber company just finished cutting. So there won't be many trees to deal with, and no one around for miles. Means we're not likely to get in trouble."

"Sounds good."

"No flying our UAVs over the water, though," she reminds me as we slide around a point and gaze at a steep hillside of ugly stumps and brush.

"For sure," I say. "Not interested in losing any equipment that hasn't been stolen already."

"We also agreed to stick to this clear-cut and not fly over private property, and to bring the drones back if any people are around."

"For real. Hey, there's that old cannery." I point beyond our intended landing site at the derelict orange-red set of buildings on old log pilings. "The one below where we were camping on the Outdoors Club trip."

"Yeah, what a mess, eh? They should take it down before it totally collapses."

I study the giant two-storey warehouse that dominates the site. It's clad in well-weathered wood and leans to one side. From the tidewater to high up on the bank, it's supported by log legs wearing barnacle-encrusted knee socks.

More pilings with moss growing out of their tops no longer hold up anything. They simply march into the bay in neat columns, like wooden soldiers with punk haircuts.

Uphill of the warehouse, a bunkhouse with a rust-streaked corrugated tin roof seems to be sliding down the bank, while even farther up, trees are bursting out of a row of roofless cottages. Throughout the property, coils of rope and tangles of fish netting intermingle with bricks from fallen chimneys and with piles of reddish boards studded by rusty nails. Broken windowpanes wink at us, backed by dark interiors, while a family of otters scurries along a warped weed-infested boardwalk that resembles a roller coaster. Ravens croak and flap as they watch us from the remains of a glass phone booth that is history frozen in time.

"Cool. We could sneak in there and explore it," I suggest.

Dorothy's paddle pauses, and she shakes her head. "My great-grandmother used to clean fish there back in the 1950s, just before it shut down. But it's falling to pieces now. Not safe to go anywhere near it. Besides, rumours are it's haunted."

She says the last few words so soberly, I have to hoot with laughter. "Of course it is!"

Her body tenses, making me wonder if she really believes in haunted cannery ruins.

She points her paddle toward barbed-wire fencing between the cannery property and our clear-cut. "Just to remind you, no letting our drones cross that line."

"Why? Who'd see them?" I tease.

"Private property. We agreed."

"Who owns it?"

"No idea. Who cares?" She shrugs.

"Okay, we agreed," I echo, thinking her tone is way too serious. Our canoe squishes into the mudbank of the Forest Service land, startling a fawn just up the ridge. Its spotted sides and tiny rump blur as it bounds away. Dorothy leaps out and ties the canoe's rope around a spindly tree beneath a house-sized boulder, then accepts the cooler and drones I hand her.

When she extends her hand to help me ashore, I keep hold of it longer than I need to, and feel tingling up and down my body when she doesn't pull away.

"Nice picnic spot," I say, pointing to a flat ledge in the sun above the giant boulder. When she nods, I lay out a blanket there and set out our sandwiches, carrot sticks, apples, drinks, and slightly squashed pieces of Mom's foil-wrapped New York cheesecake.

"Pastrami and rye, a Manhattan specialty," I boast, offering her half of mine.

"Salmon in a bun, Bella Coola specialty," she counters with a grin, offering me half of hers.

We munch and listen to birds and the lapping of waves. A white jet passes so far overhead that it's almost noiseless, coming from and going to another world. An eagle soars closer to earth, oblivious of the white curl of the jet's stream above it. The smell of cedar, salt, and moist earth swirls in the air, relaxing me, enveloping me, accepting me in my granddad's world, the place my father was born, a community now working its way

into my blood. Who'd have believed I'd ever think *that*?
I wrinkle my nose at the inlet's fishy smell, but I know
better than to complain about that to a Bella Coola girl.
My Bella Coola girl?

"Any bears likely to visit us here?" I ask lightly.

"This is the Great Bear Rainforest. We're surrounded
by them. Just keep alert. We can always jump back into
the canoe and get away."

"That's reassuring," I joke, eyeing the stump-dotted
terrain that disappears up the hill. The clearing's lack of
tall, dark trees means I'm less nervous than I usually am
outdoors.

I watch her finish off her bun, take a long sip of her
soda, and study the slope above us. She reaches for her
drone, the cherry-red midsize quadcopter sparkling in
the sun. She pops in one of her custom batteries, flicks
on the drone, and turns to me with shining eyes. Eyes
that make me want to reach out, cup her face, and kiss
her. *Nope. Not yet, Ray.*

I return her smile and pick up my slick graphite
quadcopter, Bug. Lined up on a crazy-big stump, the
drones look like they were meant to be a pair.

Dorothy gives me a playful shove to throw me off
and zips her drone up and away. Controller in hand, I
run over to get my quad in the air next to hers. Our
soaring drones seem as good at surfing the air currents
as the elegant eagles above them.

"Watch out for the eagles," Dorothy says. "They've
been known to dive down and grab small drones."

"Seriously?"

"Yeah, the army even trains some for that purpose."

"Cool. What kind of birds are the ugly black ones over there above the cannery?"

"Turkey vultures. They just feed on dead stuff. Won't mess with our birds."

"Huh," I say, eyeing the dark flock. "Never seen eagles or vultures in New York City. Just boring seagulls and pigeons. Whoa, there's like a dozen of those black vulture-things circling, Dorothy. Like they've got some prey they're about to pounce on."

"Yeah, I notice they haven't swooped in. Maybe whatever they're after is injured, not dead yet."

"You mean a suffering animal," I say grimly, steering my drone toward the hefty vultures.

"Ray! You're going over the fence! Get that thing back here!"

"Just having a quick look." I manoeuvre my baby beneath the flapping birds to see what they're eyeing. "Hey! It's a dog! Its leash is caught around a bush. It's trapped there!"

I quickly bring my drone home, and the second it lands, I sprint toward the barbed-wire fence and dive to roll under it.

"Ray!" comes Dorothy's panicked voice. "That's private property! We agreed —"

The young black Doberman, lying still on his side, has a matted coat and lesions on his throat from where he has tried to pull free of his leash. His eyes are open but half clouded over, and he flicks his paws every few seconds, as if trying to delay the moment his tormenters will drop down to push their beaks into his soft pink stomach. The leather leash is well chewed below the dog's snout, but clearly he wasn't able to work his incisors all the way through before he weakened. I unwind the leash's end from where it is caught on a thorny bush.

"Hey, boy," I say, approaching cautiously and speaking gently. *He's a Doberman and he doesn't know me, so this is dangerous*, I tell myself. But I also know he's basically too far gone to hurt me, and anyway, I'm the animal whisperer. I raise one of his ear flaps, inspect his ears, and feel behind and below them. Instinctively, I also lift his lip folds to check the colour of his gums and the condition of his teeth, jaw, and mouth.

"Gums are so dry," I mutter. I eye the bloody wounds under his collar. The poor dog's collar must have almost strangled him as he tried to free himself. "And I'm guessing blood loss leading to shock, too. Some damage to throat and trachea, perhaps? You've been here a while, haven't you? Couple of days? You look seriously dehydrated. It's okay. I'm here to help you."

I inspect the tag on his worn leather collar. *Chief*, it reads, with a local phone number. I snap a photo of it.

Dorothy's shouts fade from my awareness as I pull out my water bottle and dribble drops into the dog's parched-looking mouth. His dry tongue moves and his head stirs. Eyes as desperate as I've ever seen gaze at me in appreciation.

"Easy, Chief," I say, continuing to squirt water in his mouth as I check over his body. His eyes aren't red, I note, and the nose has no discharge, but there are lumps, bumps, and scabs on his body. "You weren't well cared for even before you escaped on your leash. And no one searched very hard for you after you disappeared." I shake my head sadly. "How dare they. Only uncaring a-holes would leave you to this."

I look up at the circling turkey vultures, black outlines with ugly red heads against the blue sky, and raise my fist at them. "Get lost!" I shout.

Then, sliding my hands beneath the big dog, I pick him up. He's heavy — I figure he weighs more than fifty pounds — but he's much lighter than he should be. He lies limp in my arms, doesn't fight me. I'm about to head back to the fence, calculating how to slide my patient under, when a spooky wail sounds from somewhere in the cannery buildings below me. The sound gets louder till I shiver involuntarily. It's a wail so pitiful and primitive and heartbreaking, I nearly drop poor Chief. I look around and register that Dorothy is out of sight and no longer calling to me.

I pause and listen hard. But now the only sounds are the breeze, seagulls calling nearby, swaying trees, and Chief's laboured breathing. There's no one and nothing else around. Even the vultures have disappeared from overhead.

"Dorothy?" I call out, my voice wavering a little.

That's when I hear the buzz of a drone directly overhead, hovering like a queen bee intent on stinging. I recognize it immediately, the same custom night-vision one that was spying on Min-jun and me when he was sleepwalking. It's yellow, it's mad, and it's big.

I run, dog bundled in my arms, till I reach the barbed wire. Gently, I kneel down, roll my patient under the fence, then press my back into the dirt to make it out after him.

Dog back in my arms, Yellow Drone retreating, I stumble downhill. When I reach our picnic site, I halt and look around in confusion. Our drones are gone, the cooler remains, I can't see Dorothy, and Granddad's canoe is no longer where we left it.

"Dorothy! Dorothy! Where are you?" I call out in panic.

CHAPTER TWELVE

WHEN I REACH the tree around which our canoe was tied, I breathe a sigh of relief. The boat has moved several feet to rest in the boulder's far shadow, and it's now upside down, but it's still on the beach and tied up. Could the tide have done all that?

I set Chief down. He watches, blinking, as I sprint up to our picnic ledge to grab the cooler and pull out my second sandwich to feed him. He snaps up the food like he hasn't eaten in days.

Looking left and right along the beach, then up-slope to the maze of stumps, I see no sign of Dorothy. Something clearly spooked her, but how far could she have gone in the short time I was away?

"Dorothy?" I shout again — and nearly soil my brand-new sweatpants as a corner of the canoe appears to lift up on its own in front of me. She's crouched beneath it.

"I'm here," she half whispers, eyes wide.

"Okay," I say, trying to calm my voice. "Did you know our drones are missing?"

"I've got them." She glances down the shoreline toward the cannery, then hands them out from under the canoe. "You brought back a dog?"

"I had to," I say. "He needs rehydrating and care at our clinic."

Dorothy shakes her head like I'm crazy but reaches for my hand and squeezes it. "You're so ... you're so *Ray*."

She crawls out from under the canoe, but I notice her trembling a little as she moves to where the boulder blocks any view of the cannery, as if she's trying to hide in the stone's shadow.

Hide from Yellow Drone, the ghost wail, or something else?

"Are you okay?" I hope my voice doesn't reveal I'm still spooked, too.

Pressing herself back into the sculpted side of the boulder, she looks at me with eyes resembling Chief's: in need of comfort, somehow. I move in and wrap my arms around her, pressing my face to her neck. She returns the hug in a fierce way, clinging to me for a full minute before taking a deep breath. "Sorry, sorry," she whispers.

Sorry for what? I'm not about to ask.

Our lips find each other's, and with a surge of warmth, my fear melts away and exhilaration seems to ride the air currents. Crickets chorus in the grass, and seawater laps joyfully at our feet. In that moment, I open myself more fully to Bella Coola.

"Hey," I say, stroking her face.

"Hey," she says, smiling and patting Chief's head as he pushes his nose between us.

Her fingers trace my jawline, then rise to my left ear. She leans in and kisses it tenderly. "Will you ever tell me the real story of your ear?"

I sigh. "I was camping with my granddad and one of his friends. I did something really stupid, and it has made me afraid of … I've never admitted this to anyone before, Dorothy, especially not to anyone in Bella Coola."

"Go on," she says, stroking that side of my head, then leaning in to offer a delicious French kiss. I'm melting into the side of the boulder, into her, but I need to finish my confession.

"I'm afraid of being alone in the woods. I'm afraid of forests, trees, wild animals. I thought maybe joining the Outdoors Club would … My granddad is always …"

"Mmm. And the something stupid was?"

I try to see it. I try to make the film advance another frame before it melts on me. "I woke up all alone in the middle of the night, in our tent. No Granddad or his friend there to protect me. There was a noise outside. I came out of the tent, and —"

"And what?"

"It's no good. It has gone all white."

"A snowstorm. They left you in a snowstorm, and you woke up and went looking for them."

I shake my head. "I don't know." I pause and think really hard till a new picture comes to me. "The next thing I remember, I'm lying on the ground with a horrible pain on the side of my head, waiting to die."

Dorothy's eyes go large, and she sits up straight. "You tried to find your granddad and his friend, who'd left you alone. You got lost and finally lay down in the snow, and your ear froze."

"I don't know," I say, exhausted from trying to access that part of my memory.

"Your grandfather and his friend found you before you froze to death?"

"Yes. Granddad found me, picked me up, and took me to the hospital."

"He must have been so relieved you were still alive!"

"Relieved?" I shake my head in confusion. "He was furious I'd come out of the tent. Told me I was useless as an outdoorsman." I take a deep breath. "Useless, Dorothy. It's why I don't fit in here. And why my granddad puts me down all the time, still."

Dorothy says, "Ray McLellan. How old were you when this happened?"

Wishing I hadn't spilled the story, I press my lips together for a moment, then go on, avoiding her question. "Don't tell Cole, Dorothy. Don't tell anyone. People already think I'm a loser. It'll be worse if they know I'm scared of the woods. That I have none of my granddad's genes. Or respect."

"Ray, answer my question. How old were you?"

"Five."

Her mouth widens. "He left you alone in a tent in a snowstorm, obviously for too long. You naturally went looking for him, and when you were nearly dead, he shouted at you for walking out to find him? You were doing what you had to. You were following survival instincts. He was the irresponsible one! He should've been arrested for child neglect! He was angry because he was ashamed, Ray. Probably out of his mind worried you'd tell your parents it was his fault. So he hammered in to you that it was —"

"— my fault." I shake my head. "You don't know my granddad, Dorothy. He was teaching me to be an outdoorsman. I knew better than to disobey him. Even at that age I could gather wood, start a fire, and read a compass. I wanted so much to be like him. Wanted him to respect me. Still do." Are those tears pushing against my eyelids? And a worried black dog pushing his nose into me? What happened to our romantic moment? I've ruined everything.

I look down at my feet. My socks and silver shoes are wet. The hem of my sweatpants is wicking water up my calves. Chief's tail is wet. I soften my voice. "The tide's coming in, Dorothy. We'd better go." I pull her close again, let my fingers run through her thick, smooth hair. "Or it will carry us away. Should we let it?"

"I'd say yes, except I'm supposed to be studying at the library."

"Um, yeah. Okay. And we have to get Chief to the clinic."

Disentangling ourselves, we right the canoe, then lift Chief inside and load up our few belongings, lashing our precious drones on top of the cooler once again.

"Nice picnic," I say.

"Yes," she says in almost a whisper, eyes reflecting the sparkle of the sun. "But we'll fly our drones somewhere else next time." She hops into the bow and waits till I shove us off before saying, "You do know that your dog stinks?"

"*Our* dog stinks," I say.

Chief's tail thumps on the aluminum bottom as I point us toward home. Dorothy and I slice our paddles through the water like we were born to it. Forty minutes? No problem with a strong girl inspiring me on — and a hostile drone behind us. Besides, I had the best two canoe instructors in the world: Granddad and Dad. So what if I'll have sore muscles tomorrow?

The smell of salt water and manky dog accompanies us all the way back to town, where Dorothy helps me lift the dog into the Jeep and the canoe on top of it. She gives me a deep kiss before springing away, saying, "I'll walk, so I can hit the library on the way home."

"Bye. Don't forget to check out a book while you're there." *But not one on paranormals or the cannery*, I'm tempted to add.

I drive home, offload the canoe, and find that Dorothy has left her jacket behind. I carry Chief into the clinic.

"Oh, poor dear!" Mom says, leaning over him instantly and doing a full body examination. "What's his story?"

"Leash got caught on a bush in the woods, and he's seriously dehydrated," I say, already setting up an IV. "Do you have time to take care of him, Mom? I'll call the owner, but I have to get to the library before it closes." To return Dorothy's jacket.

"No problem, dear. Make sure the owner can pay, though."

Halfway to the library on foot, I see Dorothy's bike disappearing into her garage. She's too far away to shout to, so I veer toward her place, intending to leave the jacket on the front porch, preferably without running into her strange old man.

I'm half a block away when I hear angry shouting coming from the garage. That's not good. Should I drop the jacket and sneak away or deliver it later — or listen in?

I sidle up to a vent on the side of the building and identify three voices plus Pilot's yapping: Dorothy, her father, and Min-jun's dad. I catch a few words: *library ... cannery ... drones ... grounded ...*

How did her father know so quickly? Since when do Mr. Kim and Mr. Dawson hang out together? And why did Dorothy lie to her father, anyway? I back away as the voices die down, and sit on a garden wall to take out my phone.

I punch in the phone number on Chief's tag. Three rings, four rings, nothing. Then a gruff voice on a recording: "You've reached Oakley and Orion Logan. Leave a message or leave us alone."

So Chief belongs to the Logan brothers. Min-jun told me two and two don't equal five, but I'm processing new math in my head right now. Mr. Dawson plus Dorothy equals Yellow Drone. I'm sure they created it, given Dorothy's reaction when I first mentioned it after the sleepwalking incident and the way she hid behind the boulder from it on our drone date. Then her dad sold it to Logan times two, who literally carried it over (staying with math-speak) to the cannery. If the cannery ghost wasn't a spirit, but an animal in pain, it might add up to Hank plus other bears multiplied. Held captive in there. An illegal, immoral bear-milking or bear-dissection operation. Oh my god! Let my wild guessing be totally wrong, please.

But I'm a vet's kid. I know an animal wailing in pain when I hear it. I just wasn't in a headspace to process the thought on that mountainside, to recognize Hank's throaty cry of desperation, or to rescue more than one animal right then. *Okay, be honest, Ray. You were scared.*

Back to the math challenge. Mr. Kim? It doesn't add up. But the final sum of the day is bad math for sure: Dorothy is in trouble because she lied to her father to spend an afternoon with me. And she was hiding from Yellow Drone because she knew its owners — the Logans — might report back the day's activities to the drone's designer, her father. A strict military man. Trespassing and taking a guard dog off private property (and kissing a guy) when she was supposed to be at the library.

I could be wrong. I could call up the conservation officer and convince him to check out the cannery property, but I've got nothing beyond a hunch, and he's already unimpressed by me. Also, he's a friend of my granddad's, and Granddad has already told me off once for sending the officer on a wild-goose chase ... er, cub chase … to the Logans' farm. I have no evidence to persuade Officer Anderson to make a trip to the old cannery as well.

Still, what if I'm right? There's one sure way to find out. And one way, maybe, to rescue Hank and any other bears held captive by a poaching ring.

My throat closes up on me as I contemplate revisiting the cannery, a mission that would require making my way into dangerous bear-infested woods. I can't do that on my own. It's pathetic to admit, but I just can't. I've flunked my outdoors training, as Granddad would be the first to point out: a weak-livered dickhead, a useless wimp. A loser city boy terrified of —

But wait. I have Min-jun as a friend — and I have a Butterfly drone, a sneaky little spy able to do almost anything in my skilled hands. If Min-jun will come with me and we can get close enough to launch a drone over the cannery property, my little Butterfly can check things out without my even trespassing.

I leave Dorothy's jacket on her front porch and manage to slink home to help with Chief before anyone emerges from the Dawsons' garage.

CHAPTER THIRTEEN

GRANDDAD IS HANGING up the phone as I walk in. From the hard look on his face, I figure something's wrong.

"That was Evan Anderson," he says. "He just found another grizzly sow carcass, bits cut out like poachers do. Plott hound and boot tracks all over the place, and her young ones gone, their trail leading to where a truck was parked." He's shaking his head.

"That's awful," I say, my teeth clenching.

"Wouldn't I love to mount the heads of bear poachers," Granddad grumbles.

"I don't blame you," I say.

"Also had a call from Jae-bum."

"Oh?"

"How was canoeing?" he asks casually. Too casually.

"Had fun," I say. "Thanks for the Jeep and canoe. Really enjoyed the paddling. Reminded me of —"

"Yer ass is grass!" he barks, eyes flashing.

From the corner of my eye, I see Mom and Dad step from the clinic into the living room, eyebrows raised at Granddad's accusation. They look from me to him.

"Excuse me?" I ask.

"I thought you were finally getting some sense in your noggin, getting some outdoors in you. But evidently your wee trip was never about canoeing, grandson, was it?"

"I took my drone along, if that's what you mean. It's best to fly it away from town, and avoid trees and people —"

"Stop pussyfooting!"

"What happened, Ray?" Dad asks. "Are you okay? Is the Jeep okay? The canoe?"

"He trespassed on private property, Jae-bum heard. The old cannery site," Granddad snarls, keeping his eyes on me.

"Oh, come on, Dad," my father says. "You did that as a youngster. I did that. Every kid around town has explored those ruins."

"Those ruins," Granddad pronounces slowly, "are way past safe like they might've been a generation ago, son, and I near enough skinned yer hide when you were caught, if you remember straight. Yer son, on the other hand, got caught on security camera footage, Jae-bum says. Which means the owners could prosecute. I s'pose you might have something to say about that, jackass?"

"Don't call my son a jackass." Mom says, face livid.

"I will if he is," Granddad says evenly.

"Leah," my dad warns.

"I'm sorry," I say, turning toward Mom and Dad. "There was a dying dog just over the fence, and —"

"The Doberman pinscher?" my dad asks. "That's where he came from? He's responding well. We treated him just in time. You did a good thing there."

Dad is standing up to Granddad? I take a deep breath and exchange looks with Mom, hardly daring to breathe. She turns back to stare at Granddad, lips pressed together, hands clenched.

"Whisht!"

That's Irish for *shush*. Granddad looks like he's going to pop a blood vessel. He shakes his head at me. "You don't trespass, steal guard dogs, and then claim they were dying, you blaggarding eejit! And you thought you wouldn't get caught? Thought yer old granddad wouldn't get a call? From people who think I can control you and yer toy-plane shenanigans? Saints preserve us! Gallivanting with a girl, no less, the Dawson lass I warned you against. Bejesus, are you trying to turn all my best customers against me? You've hardly arrived. Just grand!"

"You have a girlfriend?" Mom asks me, looking more surprised than pleased.

I've never stood up to my granddad, but something about Dorothy's earlier lecture has bolstered my nerve. "Granddad," I say with quiet authority, "just like doctors with their Hippocratic oath, veterinarians take an oath to use their skills in the best interests of animals who need their help. So it was my duty to save that dog."

"That's true, Dad," my father asserts.

A wrinkled, trembling index finger bristling with little hairs comes out from under my granddad's blanket and points straight at me.

"You — are — not — a — vet. And there'll be no more Jeep or canoe in yer life for a while. End of story. Sean, for God's sake get us a whiskey, will you, and empty this room for me?"

He sinks back into his chair, too pale and shrunken for my liking. Dad jumps to open the liquor cabinet. Mom and I back into the clinic, where the disturbance has a few patients barking, Chief not included. At least the Doberman is sleeping peacefully, destined to live a full life still.

My cell buzzes. It's a text from Dorothy: *Got caught. Grounded big time. Sorry, but can't c u 4 a while.*

I sigh and punch in, *Bummer. OK. Miss u already.*

A few days later, Mr. Kim greets me at the back door of the Korean café with a big smile, wearing a clean, starched white apron and a funny-looking hairnet. *He reports me to Granddad like a malicious town gossip, but pretends everything's cool when we meet face to face*, I think darkly.

"Ray! Good to see you! Just make kimchee mandu. You hungry?"

I've been around the Kims long enough to have developed an addiction to their cabbage, pork, and tofu dumplings, so there's no need to fake enthusiasm.

"Yes please, Mr. Kim. And is Min-jun around? I stopped by your house and Mrs. Kim sent me here."

"Min-jun!" Mr. Kim booms. He lowers a bunch of the crescent-shaped Korean dumplings into a giant fryer that sizzles and spits and sends awesome smells toward my nostrils. "Min-jun, Ray is here! You want kimchee mandu while do homework?"

"Sure, Dad." Min-jun is hunched over a small table in a far corner of the kitchen, an apron on but schoolbooks scattered in front of him, pencil poised over them. He straightens and converts a frown into a smile. "Ray! Just in time to explain our math assignment to me!"

"I can do that as long as you don't make me do dishes," I kid him.

The homework help takes ten minutes, after which we chow down the hot dumplings, then get permission to wander outside for a brief chat.

"So you and Dorothy, eh?" he teases in a hush-hush tone, elbowing me.

I turn a little red as I ask, "Where did that come from?"

"Dad was over at the Dawsons' delivering dumplings when she arrived back from your canoe trip, and somehow her dad had figured it out. As in, wasn't too happy about it."

"Mmm," I say, trying to imagine Mr. Dawson as a kimchee mandu fan, or Mr. Kim as a home-delivery guy on top of café owner and chef. "You guys don't even do takeout."

Min-jun shrugs. "What's up? Need romantic advice already, or do you have some perfect scheme for getting me off my shift tonight?"

"Just wondering if you're free this weekend."

"This weekend. There's no Outdoors Club trip, if that's what you mean, and Dad might give me a night off. But this had better not involve my quad and the Logan farm."

I laugh lightly, or try to, anyway. "Nah, just wanted someone to go camping with. Granddad isn't up to it at the moment, and my parents are too busy working. I was thinking you and me, up in the mountains. Need to take advantage of these spring days, I figure. And you can help me improve my camping skills."

He cocks his head a little and smiles. "You want to camp again, even after the last trip's disaster? Or specifically because of it, maybe? If you need a camping tune-up, I'm your man. Always good for some hiking in the hills, even during prime bear-mating season in the Great Bear Rainforest, when the bears are their most aggressive."

He's teasing me, I tell myself, so I do my best chuckle. "Perfect! Only catch is, I can't get the Jeep."

"Ah, so that's it. Unfortunately, my quad's duff right now. Needs a new CV boot. But I'll phone Cole and maybe he can get the car off his parents. So there'd be three of us. Sound good? Oh, and pack less stuff this time!"

"Um, okay. Thanks." Cole has to come with us? Damn. But oh well.

"Min-jun! Come do dishes!" his dad shouts from the back door.

"I'll text you," says my neighbour. I give him a thumbs-up and trot toward my workshop with one burning goal: to tweak my Butterfly drone so I can fly it over the cannery site on a spy mission. I have only a couple of days now to fix the drone, preferably without parts from Dorothy or her dad.

CHAPTER FOURTEEN

"THE THREE OF us are sharing a tent," Cole announces as his parents' Chevrolet bounces up the curvy road, "to make our carry-in loads lighter, and to avoid anyone being stupid." He looks in the rear-view mirror at me.

"And my dad let me come on the strict promise we won't go near the cannery," Min-jun reminds us.

Cole laughs. "All parents worry about their kids sneaking into the cannery, 'cause that's what they did when they were teenagers."

"So I'm told," I say, watching trees fly by and telling myself I'm not going to upchuck on this ride. "Think they'll ever pave these roads?"

"They're logging roads, New York." Cole's tone is taunting.

I sigh, if only to exhale the distress in my gut.

"Cole, I lied about doing bicycling and outdoors trips in New York City. The only hiking and camping I've done is with my granddad on vacations here. But I appreciate you and Min-jun being willing to join me this weekend."

So lame, but at least I'm trying to make peace with my chip-on-his-shoulder classmate.

"Ha!" Cole laughs and slams his foot down on the accelerator. The Chevy slides sideways for a second, spits loose dirt, then boots it up the winding mountainside road, stones knocking against the undercarriage like they want to get in. I close my eyes and breathe mightily through my nose, willing my stomach contents to stay where they are, knowing that Cole's eyes are locked gleefully on my pale face.

"Too bad Dorothy couldn't join us," he says. "I hear she's grounded forever. Her dad's a wacko ex-general, you know. You're lucky he didn't toss a grenade at your house."

"Whatever," I mumble. *Suck it up, Ray. He's pissed and nasty, but he has a car.*

"Don't know why you want to go back to Campsite 78," Min-jun says. "The hiking is kind of steep up there."

"I'll keep up," I vow, patting Dad's lightweight backpack with the drone hidden in its depths.

No canvas tent or army duffle this time. Nor homemade onion bagels. Because Dad helped me pack. "You got taken last time," he said with a chuckle. "Your granddad jinxed you on purpose with that ancient tent and truckload of things he called necessities. I guess Leah didn't know enough to call his bluff. Too bad I was off on an emergency call."

"Mom doesn't want me to go this weekend," I said.

"She worries," he responded casually, "but I'm proud of you for getting out with your new friends and tackling your fears head-on. You'll be fine. Let's you and me go camping next weekend if things are quiet at the clinic. Been a while, son."

As Cole's car horn blared outside, Dad gave me a rare hug and I returned it, though we both knew the clinic never calms down enough to let him go free. The clients, the sparring with Mom, and Granddad's health are all carving deep new lines on his face. As I lifted my pack, I wished I could reach up and erase them.

"We're here!" Cole announces, pulling into the dirt parking lot, which offers three entire spaces for hikers' vehicles. When I see the Forest Service Campsite 78 sign, I flash back to stumbling out of the Outdoors Club minivan, vomit pasted below my window, everyone pairing up without talking to me. This time I step out of the Chevy, welcome the fresh mountain air into my lungs, and smile at my two companions. *I can do this*, I tell myself. I'm Granddad's grandson and Dad's son, taught by the best if I'd ever bothered to listen. It's in my blood somewhere, this outdoorsman stuff. Anyway, I'm with the club's most experienced backcountry guys, and I'm doing it for Hank. If there are caged bears in that cannery, I'll be submitting photographic evidence to authorities tomorrow. Without stepping onto the property. Just sending a harmless Butterfly over the property's airspace to do the job.

We pull our gear out of Cole's trunk and distribute it between the three of us. Even if it's lighter than what I had before, it still feels like I'm hauling sandbags. We start down the trail, Cole leading, me sandwiched between my mentors. Min-jun is boasting about the tips he got last night filling in for a waiter. "Way better pay than dishwashing," he says. "And Dad's teaching me to make kimchee mandu dumplings. Watch it, guys, pretty soon I'll be top chef!"

"Scary," Cole shoots back with a real smile.

It's an hour of slogging up and down salal-choked rises before we arrive at our old camp by the stream. En route, I'm subjected to lectures on poison ivy, rattlesnakes, fire starting, and compass navigation. I don't tell them I've heard it all from Granddad before. In fact, I appreciate the refresher course.

"We did one trip with Mussett where we weren't allowed anything except a knife, bandana, cord, rain poncho, and fire flint," Cole boasts.

"No tent or sleeping bag?" I ask, figuring he's pulling my leg. "What about matches?"

"We used our rain poncho and cord as a backpack, then as a shelter. We got a fire going from the flint."

"Sounds dumb," I say, then wish I hadn't.

"It rained non-stop, and I got soaked," Min-jun said, chuckling. "Had a cold for a week after."

"Ate berries and stuff," Cole recalls. "Then one of the students stepped in real fresh bear crap."

"Yeah?" I glance at the dense woods around us and shiver.

"Mussett got his bear spray out and had us backtrack to where it was safer."

"So bear spray was allowed."

"Yeah, but you should never count on it working," Cole says seriously. "What you really need is a —"

"— five-shot capacity, forty-five-seventy high-calibre rifle. Like my granddad's," I say in a dark tone, remembering how he felled Hank's mother even though I was safely up a tree.

"He's shot plenty, all right," Cole allows. "Cougars and stuff, too. My dad has the entire body of a mountain goat mounted on his office wall, your granddad's work."

"Nice," I say without enthusiasm.

At the stream, we set up the tent, the guys for once instructing me without giving me a hard time. We lay our sleeping bags and pads in a neat row inside and hang our waterproof food bag high up between two trees, the specified height and distance from each tree trunk. Then we cram energy bars into our mouths and talk about where to hike.

"Two trails to pick from," Cole says, pointing. "Up or down, boys?"

"Down," I say before he puts it to a vote. My finger indicates the path Min-jun sleepwalked last time. I stash my water bottle and bear spray in holders on my latest belt and check the bulge in my pack that confirms the drone is there.

"I've got the first-aid kit," Min-jun tells us, "so stick with me if you're going to get injured."

"We need to all three stick tight," Cole says. "That's the agreement."

"I've got bear bells," I say.

"You know where most bear bells end up?" Cole asks in a teasing voice.

"Um, no."

"In bear scat." He and Min-jun laugh, so I join in.

Eight minutes later — I'm timing it — we pass the barbed-wire fence section that Min-jun paused near last time. Just standing near the fence that night taught us that the property is patrolled — by Yellow Drone. I look overhead and see nothing but a white osprey.

Cole and Min-jun start singing some pop song.

"You guys are so out of tune, no grizzly will come near us," I kid them.

"Viewpoint, *messieurs*," Cole announces awhile later, stepping onto a ledge and sweeping his hand across the horizon.

The panoramic view is stunning in the midafternoon sunshine. Below is the bay where Dorothy and I landed our canoe and the boulder where we kissed. My heart tugs at my chest muscles to see it. To our right is the cannery property, looking even more derelict from this height, history being swallowed by ancient forest.

I calculate the distance from where we're standing to the buildings, and decide Butterfly can make it there and back easily. "Hey, guys," I say excitedly, setting my pack down on a stump and digging into it. "I have a surprise for you."

Cole and Min-jun watch with ready grins as my drone emerges.

"Figured you might sneak one along," Min-jun says, sounding pleased. He turns to Cole. "I told you about how he flew a drone into the Logans' barn and a dog nearly ate it?"

"You're going to fly that here?" Cole asks, spreading his arms to take in all the valley and bay. "Easy to lose it, I'd think. And what for?" But I can tell he's intrigued.

"To show my friends back in the city. You think this point has a view? Wait till the drone lets us fly over the valley — virtually, of course — and see things close-up." I grab the remote controller with its mini-tablet in one hand and place the drone down on a flat rock near the edge of the cliff.

"Huh, the picture doesn't look too great there, bud." Cole points to the display on my mini-tablet. "I can hardly tell what you're looking at with that potato-quality camera."

"Bro, that's just the mini-tablet," I say with a laugh. "The better image is on my FPV goggles." I hold them up.

"What's FPV?" Cole challenges. "A freaky pervert's videocam? You use that thing in New York City to peep into high-rise apartments and stuff?"

"Negative. That would get me arrested fast," I say. "It stands for first-person view. They let me see where the drone is flying. But we can't run it anywhere that's dark, 'cause its sensor isn't thermal or anything."

"Hey, can it send secret messages to girls? Spy on enemies? How much do drones cost, anyway?" Cole asks.

"All of the above, and anywhere from fifty to fifty thousand bucks," I say. "But that's just for the drone. Doesn't include the cameras, which can cost the same or more. I designed this one myself. It's extra small. Drone operators aren't really allowed to fly them in town around people. But out here, as long as I keep it out of trees and away from the water, it —"

"— is awesome," Min-jun tells Cole. "Just try out the goggles, dude."

"Whatever," Cole agrees, shrugging.

"After I get it in the air, I'll hand you the goggles so you can see what the camera is picking up," I tell him, enjoying the way he's hovering near me impatiently.

"Then can I fly the drone?" Min-jun asks.

"Sure. But later, where there aren't so many trees."

"Okay."

They're both all but leaning into me as I launch the drone and let it drift down the slope. I veer it a little to the right over the barbed-wire fence, inching toward the cannery.

"Can I put on the goggles now?" Cole asks.

"Okay," I say, removing my FPV goggles and passing them over to Cole. I readjust to the display on my remote while cruising the drone over the property immediately below.

"Whoa." Cole takes a deep breath. "This is incredible. It's like I'm flying with the drone. Too cool! There's a deer down there!"

I manoeuvre the drone closer to the animal.

"He's looking at me! He's totally running now, and it's like I'm running with him!"

Min-jun speaks up. "I get a turn, too, right, Ray? Hey,

you're over the fence. That's private property. If you lose it over there, we can't go get it, you know."

"I won't lose it," I assure him. I buzz over the roof-less cottages, the outbuildings, and the bunkhouse, then slow over the warehouse. Aha! I steer Butterfly near a section of collapsed roof, which makes it easy to lower her into the warehouse itself. I hover in a large, near-empty space with piles of garbage in the corners. I hit the record button and spin 360 degrees, saving it all to my memory card.

"Hey, my view has gone kind of dark. Where is the drone now?" Cole asks.

"My turn." Min-jun sounds a little hurt.

"Yours in a minute, Min-jun," I assure him, taking back my FPVs from Cole so I can get a clearer view of what Butterfly is seeing.

Stacks of rusty cans, piles of fish netting, garbage, and broken chairs. Good thing my camera can't pick up smells. Must be nasty in there. I flit down a long, dark corridor and through an open door into a room with a desk and office chair. Lucky for Butterfly, the room's features are visible thanks to a skylight that's really a hole in the ceiling covered in clear plastic sheeting. As in, someone has fixed that up recently? It's hard to tell on my FPVs, but it seems like there's a dark wall of deep shelves on one side of the room.

Movement! I definitely caught something moving out of the corner of Butterfly's eye. I have my drone do a slow spin to make sure no one's there. Maybe a rat? I move my spy closer to the shelves and gasp. There's a row of padlocked cages, seven in all. Four of them contain shadows that could be bears, each moving slightly. It's too dark to identify anything more.

I turn back to the plywood desk and note scattered medical equipment: catheters, scalpels, and other instruments sitting beside a vet's first-aid kit. Behind them, a couple of muzzles hang from hooks on the wall. Finally, two coolers sit on the floor beside the desk. Do they hold food for the bears, or is it where the scum-ass poachers store the bile they pump out of the bears, to keep it cool before it goes to market?

Well, I've gotten my money shots. I've saved the views of the cages and medical stuff to my memory card. Time to get Butterfly out of the building.

I'm preparing to exit the office for the corridor when two hands grip my head and yank my goggles off. Daylight blinds me for a second.

"Hey!" I shout at Min-jun. "I said in a minute!"

But I'm too late. He's pulled the FPVs onto his face. I look at the mini-tablet on my controller in a panic. I can still manoeuvre Butterfly out of there with only that, of course. It's just more awkward.

According to my screen, Butterfly's camera is still aimed at the desk, turned away from the cages. Min-jun is seeing nothing but the desk chair with a coat slung over it, and maybe a corner of the first-aid kit. Phew! I zip Butterfly through the open doorway and down the long hallway to the warehouse's open space, then perform lift-up through the collapsed roof and order my spy home. She soars back to us up the slope.

But Min-jun and Cole are rolling on the ground at my feet, Min-jun tearing at the goggles on his face. Cole's on top of his friend one minute, then dragging him by the boots away from cliff's edge the next.

"Guys!" I shout. "Stop fighting over my goggles!"

"What's wrong with him?" Cole gasps as I retrieve Butterfly from where she lands. "I thought he was going to pull us both over the cliff."

"Min-jun?" I say. "Sorry, I got carried away. Your turn. You want to fly it now?" I put Butterfly on the ground beside him, hoping he's not mad at me.

That's when I notice he remains face down on the ground and is jerking from head to boot.

"You okay, Min-jun?"

He closes a fist around Butterfly, raises his arm, and smashes my baby down on a rock. His knuckles come up bleeding.

"Min-jun!" I cry out.

"What the —?" Cole backs away like he's freaked, and looks to me with an open mouth.

I leap forward and press my chest down on Min-jun's back. At the same time, my right palm closes around his, and as his body bucks, I forcibly remove my drone. Then, like I did before, I wrestle him onto his side, check his breathing, and anchor his thrashing limbs.

"It's an epileptic seizure," I tell Cole.

But did he break the drone accidentally, or on purpose?

"Wha-a-t?" Cole says.

"Stress can set off people with epilepsy," I say, more to engage Cole and keep him calm than to inform him.

"It'll be over in a few minutes. Then we'll need to let him rest till he comes to. What's most important, though, is to act like nothing happened. Don't mention it. He'll be very embarrassed."

Cole's still staring at the two of us, his jaw unhinged. "And you know this because …?"

"I'm a vet's kid."

"Huh. Mussett definitely did not cover this in his camping first-aid course."

When Min-jun's body finally goes still, I wrap my coat around him. He's not fully aware yet.

"He could've died if you … and he wrecked your drone, didn't he?" Cole mumbles.

I grit my teeth and reach for it. "I can fix it, but today's film is toast."

"Oh," Cole says. "At least it's just shots of cannery ruins."

Cannery ruins with something that freaked out Min-jun, I think grimly. What did he see? And will he even remember?

CHAPTER FIFTEEN

IT'S DARK BY the time we've hauled Min-jun back to camp and eased him into his sleeping bag. Cole makes me gather wood and start the campfire to show I can do it, and we eat heated-up baked beans in silence, the sound of frogs and crickets accompanying the scrape of our spoons.

"You wanted to camp here to get drone shots of the cannery, didn't you? Why? It's just a heap of rotting wood," he says.

"Thought my friends in New York would find it interesting," I lie again, unwilling to share my poaching-ring suspicions with my moody camping mate.

"Nothing inside but garbage and graffiti," he says. "Been there lots of times. It stinks," he adds, scrunching up his nose and taking a swig of his soda. "Not worth losing your drone for."

"Yeah," I agree, though the image of the shadow-crammed cages in that dark corner and medical tubing on the table makes me want to charge down there right now and free the bears.

"Is it true you found a half-dead guard dog there and fixed it up in your clinic?"

"Does everyone in Bella Coola know everything that goes down in Bella Coola five minutes after it happens?"

"Count on it, New York."

"Yes. A Doberman pinscher. Belongs to the Logan brothers."

"Logan brothers," Cole says with distaste. "Stay away from those two."

"Why?"

He shrugs and finishes his drink. "Let's clean up and check on Min-jun."

We scrub our dishes carefully, then pack away the rest of the food in the food bag and rehang it between the two trees. It swings in the air like a punching bag on a clothesline.

"That's safe. No bears are going to reach it, no matter how hungry they are," Cole says with satisfaction. "Promise me you have no food stuff in the tent. Not even toothpaste."

"Not even toothpaste," I pledge. "I have no interest in a bear visit tonight."

"For sure," he says. "'Cause they're really hungry, aggressive, and unpredictable this time of year, especially with cubs around."

Including cubs that are being kidnapped, I think with a shiver. But I'll put a halt to that, somehow.

"At least it's not hunting season yet," he adds as we douse our campfire and crawl into the tent beside Min-jun.

Except for poachers, I reflect. Granddad and I agree on their heads needing to be mounted.

I dream that night of UAVs flying over our tent, buzzing like a formation of Amazon delivery drones. Yet somehow their approach feels sinister. They hover a few feet from the tent, then open their claws to release their loads, one after another. Not packages, but grenades. A mad general is at the controls, yahooing each time he drops one. "That'll teach you to date my daughter!" he cackles. Then the UAVs lift up and away and disappear into the silent night.

Cole shakes me awake. It's still dark.

"Shhh," he whispers. "Grizzlies in our campsite."

Grizzlies? As in plural? My left ear buzzing, I rocket out of my sleeping bag and feel around for my can of bear spray. Cole's hand closes over my wrist. "Shhh."

Min-jun's awake now, and Cole warns him in whispers, leaving him wide-eyed. Only Cole's headlamp is on, just enough to reveal panic on all our faces. We're on our knees, still as statues, facing the zipped-up tent door like condemned prisoners awaiting execution. Min-jun has an open penknife in his hand. Cole and I poise trigger fingers above spray cans.

At the sound of grunts outside, adrenalin crackles through my system like neon lighting. I shuffle forward and unzip our tent an inch. I put my eye to the hole, then choke on fear and slide back on my knees.

Cole moves to the peephole. When he sits back on his butt, his face is drained of colour.

The grunts get louder, along with slurping and thumping as they fight over the food. A foul smell drifts right through the tent walls and makes me lift my T-shirt to my face to breathe through it. Did they wrestle our bear bag down after all? Tear it open and invite all their friends over? Will we be dessert?

Min-jun takes his turn looking and scrambles backward. *Please don't have another seizure now,* I think.

We sit motionless for the better part of an hour, hardly daring to take sips from our water bottles. As dawn creeps through the tent sides, I expect a giant clawed paw to tear into the thin nylon at any moment, and a stampede of bears to trample us, close jaws on us, feast on us.

"Leave 'em alone an' they'll usually leave you alone," Granddad likes to say. "They prefer berries and salmon to people."

Salmon. That's the smell. They've pulled fish from the stream beside us and are having a banquet. But why not do it on the stream bank instead of beside our tent?

Grunts and snuffling fill our ears. Then we feel the earth shake as they move away. We allow for a good twenty minutes of silence, not counting the reassuring morning bird sounds, before we peek and confirm the coast is clear.

"I say we move on out of here now that there's enough light," Cole suggests. "I'm okay with calling off hiking today. Min-jun?"

"Definitely. This campsite's not safe, and I'm really tired, anyway."

Cole and I exchange glances, but don't bring up the seizure incident. Nor am I about to say anything about my broken drone. It's fixable. But is Min-jun's condition? Either he lied to me about how frequent his seizures are, or they're increasing.

We crawl slowly out of the tent, one by one, like cartoon characters waiting for bad guys to spring on us. Almost tiptoeing around the stinky mess of salmon heads and bones, under the gaze of ravens wanting the leftovers, we pee in the stream. There isn't a single salmon visible in its waters or on its bank, which is several long strides from our tent.

After voting not to take the time to cook up our instant oatmeal, we lower the intact bear bag, push our sleeping bags into their stuff sacks, pack up the tent faster than ace army recruits, then double-check that the campfire is cold. As we start up the trail to the parking lot, nervously eyeing the shadowy forest around us, we sing loudly and badly, me jingling my bear bells like it's Christmas at Madison Square Garden. Only when the Chevy's doors have slammed shut and Cole has turned over the ignition do we breathe freely.

"Why did they drag the salmon into the campground?" Min-jun asks what each of us has been turning over in our minds. "Did you guys leave anything around that attracted them?"

"Negative," I say for both Cole and me.

"I didn't know there were any salmon in that stream," Cole says in a puzzled voice, "never mind this early in the year."

"It's like someone dumped a pile of salmon next to us in the middle of the night while we were sleeping, to bring the bears around," I say.

Cole laughs shakily. "Good one."

"But there were no boot prints except ours. I checked," Min-jun says.

"You checked for foreign boot prints to see if someone brought us a breakfast special?" Cole tries to mock Min-jun, but I can see in the mirror that he's frowning. Silence follows.

"I heard drones in the middle of the night," I finally say. "I heard them dropping stuff next to the tent."

Maybe I was dreaming, maybe I wasn't. It's the only explanation. Yellow Drone and its poacher operators wanted to scare us away after catching me filming the cannery. Their UAV is large and easily strong enough to dangle a few pounds of salmon for a mile or two as the crow flies. As a drone flies. Over enemy lines.

Cole brakes suddenly. He pulls over on the side of the gravel road to twist his head around and direct bug eyes at me.

"Are you serious?" he asks.

"Yes," I say, looking to Min-jun for support. Min-jun saw something inside the cannery yesterday. He also saw the stealth drone on the Outdoors Club camping trip. Does he remember either? Both? He might make the connection. Instead, he chuckles like it's a great joke.

"You are whack, Ray," Cole pronounces in a cold voice. "You know nothing about bear country, salmon, or Bella Coola. You move here, try to take our girls, pretend you know about the great outdoors. You lied about wanting to learn camping tips, when all you really wanted was a ride here to fly your stupid toy. I knew you were a drone nut, but I didn't know you were a paranoid lunatic. Sure — drones came by in the night to drop off salmon. Min-jun, I say we get him to the hospital right now, so they can put one of those special white jackets on him and lock him away."

His eyes bore into me, and I see all his resentment for my single date with Dorothy burning like dangerous embers.

"Guess you don't get my sense of humour," I say in a tone unconvincing even to myself. "Sorry if you thought —"

"We're out of here, Min-jun," Cole declares, pulling back onto the road and making like a derby racer. "And don't even think of signing up for another Outdoors Club trip," he warns me, even though he's vice-prez, not prez.

Min-jun is looking out the window, frowning like he wants nothing more to do with the conversation. Anger rising, in need of some kind of revenge, I can't stop myself from breaking my code of silence about the seizures.

"Min-jun," I say testily. "You said you have seizures every couple of months. But yesterday's makes at least two in one month. Are your episodes increasing?"

He studies the woods flashing by like he hasn't heard me. Cole glances at his friend but says nothing.

"Because if they're increasing, that's called pre-stasis. It's super serious. You could have a seizure you don't recover from. You could die."

I see him swallow, see his jaw go tight.

"You need to see a doctor, Min-jun. You need different medication or a change in how much you're taking."

When he finally speaks, it's hardly loud enough for me to hear. "I'm taking something. My dad has upped the dosage. And it's none of your business."

Cole speaks up, startling me. "It's our business if you kick the bucket on one of our camping trips. But maybe it's our business just because we care." His tone is gentle, in sharp contrast to when he addressed me earlier.

"Western medicine or traditional Chinese medicine, TCM?" I dare to ask.

Min-jun turns my way in surprise, glares at me, then slumps in his seat. "The medicine the Bella Coola doctor gave me had bad side effects. And my dad won't let me go back there because a cousin of his who was really sick died after taking Western medicine. My mom and dad argue about it, but I'm going with what my dad gives me. Now leave me alone," Min-jun says in a dejected voice, and he all but pastes his face against the car window.

It's not the right time to argue with him, I figure. And anyway, traditional medicines have been used forever in other cultures, so who am I to diss them, as long as there's no cruelty to animals involved? Even if Western science doesn't understand traditional medicines, or hasn't tested them all, they're gaining respect and evidence these days — in veterinary as well as people medicine.

As the car jolts from pothole to curve, I imagine us arriving home and Min-jun's dad instantly phoning Granddad to tell him that I flew my drone into the cannery. Also that I left something around our campsite that attracted bears in the night. I imagine Cole's dad, a taxidermy customer of Granddad's, confirming it.

"Count on it," Cole had said earlier. Everyone knows everything within five minutes. Even though I've kept mum about Min-jun's seizures till now.

"Guys," I say, and they turn slightly toward me. "Can we agree that what happened at Campsite 78 stays at Campsite 78?"

The car bounces around two hairpin turns before they respond.

"Agreed."

"Deal."

We'll see if their word is good.

CHAPTER SIXTEEN

SINCE BEING DROPPED off by Cole, I've put in five phone calls to Evan Anderson and made one visit to his office. No one there, and no replies. Just a recorded message that refers emergency calls to the police. I'm pissed and anxious. I could write him a note or leave him a long message, but what do I really have that would convince him? No film anymore, damn it. Nor anyone else who saw the same thing I did.

"Grandson," Granddad starts in during dinner, "how was camping with Min-jun and the other fellow?"

"Good," I say, braced for a harangue.

"I hear you did everything perfectly: tent pitching, fire starting, bear-bag hanging. Did yer family proud for once." He spoons up Mom's Manhattan clam chowder with gusto.

"Mmm," I say, still waiting.

"And grizzlies, eh? You saved yer mates from harm by keeping 'em quiet, helping 'em keep their heads on. Quite the hero, is how Min-jun told it to his dad."

"Grizzlies?" Mom's spoon halts halfway to her mouth. She looks from Granddad to Dad to me.

"We were a safe distance away," I say cautiously. "Just watched them eat salmon."

Dad smiles. "It's bear country, honey, like I keep telling you. Great chowder, by the way."

"Three young boys camping alone overnight, and the fact that they encounter bears doesn't worry you?" she challenges my father. "How many bears, Ray?"

I hesitate, but decide to tell the truth. "Six, including the cubs."

Dad gives a quiet sigh and throws me a look like, *Don't fan the flames, please.* He also looks a little startled at that number.

Granddad grins as he scrapes his bowl clean. "Sean here was eight the first time he camped on his own with a schoolmate."

"You mean in the backyard?" Mom asks Dad.

"Probably," Dad says, tossing his father a look.

"Nope. Up in the mountains. His mom and I, we picked 'em up in the morning. You two were banjaxed but big-eyed happy," he recalls.

"Eight years old? Without adult supervision?" Mom's spoon clatters to the table. "But that time no one lost an ear from your irresponsibility, did they?" Her eyes narrow at Granddad.

"Honey," Dad says, reaching for her hand.

"Yer not from here," Granddad says, like he's delighted to have gotten a rise out of Mom. "Kids learn woodsmanship early in these parts. They learn to coexist with nature. Boys grow up to be men, not like in the city."

I groan inwardly and feel my entire body tense up. Mom can be like a pit bull sometimes, not knowing when to back down. And Granddad likes to bait.

"Oh, so you're in charge of Ray's manhood now, are you?" she asks, although Dad has risen and put his hands on her shoulders like he's about to lead her away from the table.

"He just came back a hero today, Leah," Granddad all but spits out at her. "He's earning his spurs. He's a McLellan."

Compliments from Granddad? I'd go into shock if I didn't realize he was working some kind of agenda.

"Okay, Dad, we're all proud of Ray, but let's leave it at that," Dad says. "It's been a long day."

"It has been a long month," my mother says, voice steady and alarmingly hollow as she stands and places her napkin in the centre of the table, "with your father always interfering in family matters, insulting me, bullying Ray, and complaining about our clinic, which pays for all the meals I make him, which he never thanks me for, not once. And you, Sean, I never knew how spineless you were till we moved here. Never sticking up for Ray or me." Her voice goes spookily soft. "Your father is a bully and I'm tired of living under the same roof as him."

A pain in the back of my throat grows to tonsillitis level. Granddad rises unsteadily, almost triumphantly, and points his finger at her. "Then git!" he pronounces. "Git out o' my house. Now! Had more than enough o' yer whining!"

"Dad, stop it!" Dad shouts, as I shrink into my seat. "Leah!" But she has walked dead calmly into their bedroom and shut the door softly. Dad throws a sad glance at Granddad, but before Dad can make a move, I cross the room, boldly slip into the bedroom, and close the door behind me.

Mom is sitting on the bed, her back to me, trembling slightly. I take a shaky step forward and sit down beside her. Her arm reaches out and I grasp her hand. She smells like lilac soap.

We sit together awhile as her breathing steadies.

"Mom ..."

She pats my hand as I retreat back into silence.

"I'm ... I'm sorry," I say. Huh? For what? For the way I've only been thinking of myself, not her? For how Granddad treats her, for Granddad's illness, for how Dad is caught in the middle? For how I'm all twisted up inside, trying to ignore it all? I need to spend more time with her, do more for her.

"I'm sorry I ... I've never really thought before how hard it is on you. I mean, *he's* hard on you. For sure. Granddad, I mean. Sometimes I want to blow up, too, but ... Well, if anyone gets to, it's you." Yet she didn't. Maybe in words, but not in tone. She's a strong woman. She's my tenacious mother.

Her body shudders a little and she raises a hand to wipe away an escaped tear. *Not helping, Ray.*

"But we can't change Granddad, and Dad's trying his best. What I really want to say is —"

She turns to me and draws me into a fierce hug. The kind I haven't had since I was little. A long hug that feels good, and which I return as I mumble, "I love you."

There's a soft knock on the door, and Dad peers in, a solemn look on his face.

"I'll do dishes," I say, rising quickly to leave them alone.

I clear the table without looking at my granddad. I'm still warm from Mom's hug, and that makes me hope things will be all right. It's true I've been so into my own stuff that I haven't really thought about how Mom has been struggling. What can I do about that? Granddad can be a pain, especially to her. On the other hand, he's family, and I can't toss away my loyalty to him, especially as his health gets worse. I also feel sorry for Dad, who's in the centre of a tug-of-war between two stubborn people he loves: homesick Mom and grumpy Granddad. A contest that can have no winner. He's not handling it perfectly, but can't Mom see he's doing his best?

Like Dad, I just want peace. And somehow, with every day that goes by, I'm less interested in moving back to New York. I'm not sure why, but it's not just Dorothy. Bella Coola can grow on a person.

I soap each plate like I'm treating a skunked dog, slow and steady. Only when I've finished washing the dishes do I turn. Granddad is attempting to make his own way from the table to his bedroom, in serious danger of falling and breaking bones. I rush over and offer him an arm. He takes it, pats it, and lets me help him to his bed, where he waves me away before collapsing onto his frayed quilt. He looks small and shrunken now, all the fight drained away. His skin isn't a healthy colour, and his hands shake as he arranges his pillow.

"Good night, Granddad," I say as I back out of the room.

"Night, Ray."

I hesitate at the door. "Granddad?"

"Yes, Ray?"

"You know the Forest Service Campsite Number 78?"

"I know all the campsites within a ten-mile radius."

"Do salmon swim up the stream there?"

"That wee pisser? Never in a million years, grandson. Anyway, most salmon don't spawn 'round here till fall, which you'd know if you ever listened to me."

The following afternoon, Mom picks me up from school with Chief in the back seat.

"Hey, Chief," I say fondly, reaching through the window to scratch his head. I'm wondering why Mom has shown up, rather than letting me walk home like usual. Not that I mind a ride. I hardly slept last night. And today felt like the first miserable day of school all over again. Dorothy gave me no more than one sad nod from far away. Cole avoided me altogether, and I saw him chatting with Dorothy twice. Trying to move in already? Min-jun was absent, as in sick. I spent lunch hour by myself, phoning Officer Anderson over and over again, and getting nothing but his mailbox-full and police-referral message.

Mom's all dressed up in heels and a nice dress that look totally out of place in the driver's seat of the dusty Jeep. I haven't seen her since the intense dinner spat last night.

"Hi, Ray," she says, over-the-top chirpy.

"Hi," I say. It comes out strangely, like a question mark.

"Time to return Chief to his owners. Thought you might like to ride along."

I'm tempted to bolt rather than climb in. The last people I need to see right now are the Logan brothers. Instead, I sigh, seat myself, and fasten my seatbelt. I'll just stay in the vehicle and let Mom return Chief and do the talking.

"I'll miss you, Chief," I tell him over my shoulder.

We head up the hill in awkward silence.

"Ray, you should know that I'm flying to Vancouver tonight."

"You're what?" My stomach turns over.

"Tomorrow I'll fly on to New York City."

I shake my head and curl my fingers into my palms. "When are you coming back?"

"Dad will join us when he's ready."

"Us?" My teeth clench.

"There's room on the flight tonight. I checked. We can spend a day in Vancouver if you like. Eat sushi and find some live music and ..." Her voice falters. "I think it's safe to say the stint here hasn't worked out. It won't be a big deal for you to slip back into your old school this week. Your friends will be delighted, and you can help me in the clinic as much as you like. We'll release the vets we rented it to. I'll need your help till Dad comes."

She seems to think that the faster she talks, the more likely it'll all happen like she's saying. My spine is so tight it's about to snap.

"Jae told us your girlfriend broke up with you. Sorry about that, honey."

She wasn't my girlfriend, and now she never will be, I think.

She reaches out to touch my hand, but I pull it out of her reach.

"Ray?" She pulls up to the Logan brothers' property, in front of the wire gate that's padlocked shut.

I picture Arlo and Koa grinning big, whisking me with them to Central Park for a drone-flying session first thing. I imagine them ogling my newest invention. My mind scans all my favourite New York eateries, cinemas, sports stadiums. I feel the throbbing excitement of the city that truly never sleeps. I remind myself that Mom and Dad never fought in the city, only here under Granddad's roof. Then I look around me at the Great Bear Rainforest and breathe in the peace and the cedar scent. An image of Dorothy hovers at the edge of my view.

"Don't do this, Mom," I say, a flood of tears threatening to burst from behind my eyeballs. "New York's not home anymore. This is home, right here. With Dad. You can learn to like Bella Coola. I have." Dorothy, Min-jun, the valley views, almost everything has grown on me. I run a sleeve over my face, then start as Chief leaps up and barks in the back seat.

Oakley Logan, wearing — surprise, surprise — a logging shirt, camo trousers, and army boots, is peering through the gate, then unlocking it. He's also squinting at my wet face. "Aww, the kid is *that* attached to Chief?" he says in a mocking tone. "Come on, Chiefie. You're lookin' good. They spoil you at that clinic?"

Mom gets out, opens the back door, and lets Chief leap out, tail wagging.

"Oakley Logan," he says, extending his hand. "Man, if I knew you was in the vet office, I'd've come visitin' way 'fore now."

Mom stiffens and shakes his hand curtly.

"Jist kiddin'. Went to school with Sean, y'know. We was buddies 'fore he got all snobbish and urban. Used to be a wildman like me, y'know. Not." He winks.

She's busy searching her purse for the invoice.

Getting no reply from her, Oakley spits on the ground and lifts his John Deere baseball cap at me. "Little McLellan again, is it? You still don't remember, eh, but we went campin' together with your grandfather. He and I go way back, son. Been huntin' and fishin' and makin' trouble together since 'fore you was born."

I study him closer, and a memory stirs. My left ear tingles. I see him sitting beside the campfire with my granddad, the two of them cooking hot dogs. I'm five. *The* camping trip. But the snapshot fades just as fast. I shrug, humiliated he just saw me leaking tears that had nothing to do with Chief.

"Whoohee!" Oakley exclaims as Mom hands him the vet bill. "But no prob. This old boy's worth it, hey, dog? Lost him while hikin' in the mountains."

He's making way too much of a show, petting his Doberman. Makes me sick, knowing how he really treats his hound. Nor do I believe he lost the dog while hiking. I look around behind him, half expecting to see stacked cages or chained-up bears, but it's just a farm gone to seed, with a tumbledown barn and outbuildings.

"I hope you'll treat him better than someone did before he was found," Mom says sternly.

"You bet, ma'am." He pulls a few crisp hundred-dollar bills out of his wallet. Mom's plucked eyebrows rise. Who carries that many hundreds around? But she's cool and professional as he hands her the fee in cash, plus a tip.

"Thanks agin," he says, lifting his John Deere cap a second time.

"Son," he adds, eyes narrowing slightly, maybe because of the sun. "Take care of that there granddad of yours. Or is it true you're headed home to the big smoke now, like your granddad jist tol' me on the phone?" With a click, the gate's padlock closes, and without a backward glance, Oakley and a fully mended Chief trot away.

I take a deep breath and bite my tongue. Everyone knows everything around here, within minutes. Count on it.

"Well," says Mom, gazing at the money in her hand. "At least he paid up."

She spins like she's about to get back in the Jeep, then frowns as she takes in my slumped figure. She walks over in her high heels and embraces me. "You and me," she whispers. "We're a team. Let's have some city fun before Dad comes home."

I rip myself away from her before the floodgates open. "No!" I shout, running down the hill. "You can't force me to choose between you and Dad, or here and the city!"

I veer away from the road so she can't see me, can't follow me. *She'll change her mind*, I tell myself. She was just testing me. She'll forgive Granddad. He'll lay off her. Dad will convince her to stay. I won't witness my family's breakup.

Biting my tongue, I also decide I won't go back to the log cabin. I'll do what I've been intending to do all day: hide in my workshop and finish my night-vision drone, Skyliner. Then head to the cannery, with or without Officer Anderson, and rescue Hank. He's back to being my only friend in Bella Coola.

I work much of the night, dozing off just once. Dad begs me to come in, then brings me a sandwich. His face looks grey and long. He drags his feet as he walks, like Min-jun in his sleep. I wait for Mom to U-turn on her ride to the airport, show up here in my workshop. Surely she'll take my hand, beg forgiveness, and lead me to supper. When I hear Bella Coola's last flight south lift up overhead, I tell myself Mom's not on it. Or if she is, then one day in Vancouver, or a week in New York, and she'll return for us. She knows it's wrong.

It's unfair. It's a hurtful, unreasonable, inexcusable, rash, imprudent, dumb-assed mistake. Reversible. The plane will turn around. Can I send all my drones up into its flight path to force it down? Not. At least I've repaired Butterfly, who sits pretty on the shelf beside Bug, watching me work on my drone number three.

At 3:30 a.m., I lift my thermal camera and attach it to the gimbal that now forms its underbelly. "You're looking a little chubby, dude," I tell it. "But you're finished! Finally!"

Dripping with tiredness, heart pounding, nerves on edge, I place my precious bundle under my arm and tiptoe into the house. There, I grab a jacket, some snacks, and the Jeep's key. In the clinic, I grab some sedative pills to ease Hank's pain. Next, I slip into the garage and load up a life jacket, a paddle, a headlamp, and some bear spray — even a small pair of bolt cutters for good measure.

It's 4:15 and still pitch-black when I slide the canoe onto the Jeep's racks without a single squeak. Grounded? Can't use the Jeep or canoe? Try to stop me, old man. You just tore our family apart the way a split nucleus creates an atomic bomb explosion. I hope the guilt kills you while I'm away. You think I can't walk through the woods by myself? Think I'm scared of trees? You are so wrong. You're wrong, nasty, evil, and manipulative.

My ear begins spitting sparks of pain. I clamp my hand over it. You took my ear away. I don't know what happened, but it was never my fault, was it? You took my mother away. You probably even ordered your friend Evan Anderson not to call me back.

Tears are running down my face as I back out of the garage and drive to the town's boat launch. There's not another set of headlights on the road. I ease the canoe off at the ramp, then park the Jeep, knowing there's a spare key under the back bumper for someone to return it home. Let them report me lost or a runaway. They'll never find me in the Great Bear Rainforest, which is the size of West Virginia. It's bigger than Nova Scotia. It's like one and a half Switzerlands, according to one tourist brochure.

I'm about to step into the canoe when I notice a small camouflage motorboat tied up nearby. Has to be the one I saw with my binoculars the first day of the Outdoors Club trip. I can still picture it slipping under the cannery dock. I wander over and look into it. Nothing to mark it as suspicious. Just a small outboard motor, and oars with oarlocks. But it could belong to the poachers! Disabling it would slow down their operation, right? I wrestle with my conscience for a minute, glance around, then manhandle the motor off the stern and dump it in the woods behind. Wiping sweat from my brow, and fighting off the guilt, I toss branches on top of the motor, then return to haul the oars under a nearby fallen tree for good measure.

Far to the east, a grey stripe announces the coming day. I climb into my getaway canoe, plunge my paddle into the dark water, and move forward while keeping close to shore, where bears, cougars, wolves, and wolverines watch with glowing eyes and crouch, waiting to pounce. But not on me, not today.

CHAPTER SEVENTEEN

WIND WHIPS AGAINST my life jacket, and waves ricochet off the sides of the canoe, but I'm a man on a mission, unswampable. My biceps and pecs, or lack thereof, pull and pull some more. My tongue tastes both salt water and sweat. Grey seagulls swoop overhead. Before me lies a breathtaking panorama of glaciated mountains, river, inlet, and trees. Endless trees. I love trees.

I remember Dad and Granddad making me my first wooden paddle, helping me stain it, showing me how to pull it through the sparkling water of this same bay. *Despite vacationing here only once a year, I'm a Bella Coolan of sorts*, I tell myself, *and maybe a McLellan after all.*

I know more, am capable of more, than I give myself credit for, or than Granddad would ever admit. I can be both outdoorsman and urban, Granddad, as surely as my mother's blood pulses in me along with yours and Dad's. Then there's my mother's temper plus your temper: a helluva combo to inherit. Together they make me stubborn and determined enough to be heading for the cannery right now.

As dawn makes the sky flame pink, I eye the approaching huddle of sagging buildings, but give them a wide berth and pass on by, so as not to arouse suspicion. I'll override my fears to set up in the dense woods beyond, well off cannery property but within drone-flying distance of it. We'll go undetected, me and my squadron: Bug, Butterfly, and Skyliner. I'll direct one or more to buzz in, get the shot this time, and fly out. Then it's up to the cops or conservation officer. I'll let them shut the operation down. Mom, Dad, and I will look after the rescued bears when they're released. Wait, Mom's gone. My parents have split up. *Ray, keep your mind on beaching the canoe.*

I manage to push my bow between two barnacle-covered boulders. As I leap out and pull on the canoe's lead rope, I wet my hiking boots and the hem of my new slim-fit cargo pants — yes, I've dressed down for the day, or maybe it's my new look. Finally, I turn the boat over and sink down on it, shivering in the cool morning air.

I almost bolt back to the water when I hear something scramble along a branch two storeys above. Picturing a bear about to drop down and maul me, I raise my face and cover my throbbing ear. Two black, beady eyes peer back from that perch. Oh my god. I'm about to reach for my bear spray when the creature's funny-looking head moves more clearly into view. *Okay, idiot. It's a porcupine*. But from a distance, porcupines look just like bear cubs with bad haircuts.

"Boo," I shout at it, aiming a pinecone upwards. The creature skitters along the branch toward the tree trunk and disappears. Good riddance to him. I've pulled quills out of way too many dogs on my vacations here to feel kindly toward the prickly creatures. Peering at the rough bark of another tree trunk, I wonder if I'm going crazy. It's literally rippling in the grey light. I move toward it, then leap back. An army of ants, rushing in streams like Grand Central Station commuters.

Stop wasting time, Ray. Get a grip. Fly a drone.

Of course, locating a spot that offers clearance overhead for my drones is a challenge. No Min-jun or Cole to help me, no Granddad to micromanage me. It's okay, because I can do this.

Still, I'm overwhelmed by a need for companions, preferably last week's camping mates. Then I remind myself they're pretty much ex-mates since I opened my stupid mouth about drones carrying salmon to our campsite. Did I really expect them to buy that? But maybe, just maybe, it'll make some sense to them later. They've grown up here. Surely they'll realize that the salmon couldn't have come from our site's stream. Nor do bears drag their dinner into an occupied campsite before eating it.

I pack up my three drones, my remote controller, FPV goggles, a snack, the headlamp, and the binoculars in my backpack, and double check that my bear spray and water bottle are on my belt. Finally, I pat my cargo pants pockets, which contain the handful of sedatives for Hank, my phone, and the bolt cutters.

Good to go. I wander uphill, my heart pounding like a New York City jackhammer. Twigs crackle underfoot, while above me, old branches rub, creak, and threaten to break and fall on my head. Some of the larger trees sport enormous toe-like appendages where they meet the ground, while their roots snake over the entire forest floor, plotting to trip me up. The dew on the endless ferns wets my calves, neon-bright moss makes for slippery walking even in my new woodsman boots, and tiny creatures scurrying in the undergrowth are making this walk a freak-out fest.

I'm on high alert for bears, terror shadowing my every footfall. Indeed, the forest seems to close in on me by the minute. Maybe this is dumb. Maybe I should have stayed home. No. Home isn't home anymore. And I'm here to help Hank.

My breath leaves me when I see a large shadow up ahead. I freeze behind a three-foot-wide fir tree.

I note the silver-tipped hump, the barge-sized feet, and the teddy-bear ears. It's definitely a grizzly, and it seems to be in happy mode. Crouched with front paws crossed neatly beside a stream's muddy patch, it keeps poking its nose into the water and blowing bubbles, then popping them with an ursine bite. Like a kid at bath time.

Now he — definitely a "he," I can see now — rolls in moss like he's having all the fun in the world, but soon moves to an indentation on the hill and lies down like a tired child, rubbing his tummy and wiggling his nose like it's nap hour. Taking his time, he scratches his sides with his hind feet, gives himself a chest massage with all four paws, and finally rubs his face with his front claws. I watch him dig, presumably for insects, then shake his shaggy coat and swagger to a tree.

I'm smiling. He's so, well, *human*.

He rears up, his back to the tree, and rubs it like he needs a back scratch. Mussett told us about bear-rubbing trees. During mating season, the guys do it to leave their scent so the girls they're after know they're around and looking. They also do it to let the other guys know their territory — like dogs pee to mark theirs, and human gangs spray graffiti tags. Granddad told me cubs sometimes rub on the same trees to pick up an aggressive male's scent, so that he's less likely to kill them. Smart kiddos.

There's no way I'm going to accidentally surprise this one, like I did Hank's mother. I've learned a thing or two since then. Gotta stay at least 250 feet away: the wingspan of a 747.

I try to imagine a 747 between me and the beast, who's moving up and down like he's practising dance moves. My damaged ear is producing so much static, I'm afraid the grizzly is going to hear it. I'd love to climb into the imaginary 747 and fly out of here, but that's not going to happen. I could stand here ready to spray him, or dive to the ground and lock my hands around my face and neck, or —

Climb a tree, Ray. You can. You've got time. You've done it before.

Heart pounding, I notice how the fir offers low footholds. I'm about to scramble up when it occurs to me to
leave Bug at the tree's base. I can operate it from higher
up, but maybe not launch it from some narrow branch
without crashing it. So, after setting Bug down like a
garden elf, I put foot against bark and begin to climb.
Higher and higher I go, stomach knotted like a New York
pretzel, hands catching and bleeding on rough branches,
boots occasionally slipping. At least I ditched the silver
running shoes, a useless souvenir of … well, of that city
my cowardly Mom is heading toward this minute.

One story, two storeys, three storeys above the forest
floor. *No falling from here*, I order myself. I'm upwind
of looking-for-romance Stud Griz, who seems to have
taken no notice of me. *Grizzlies can but usually don't
climb trees*, I remind myself. Except as cubs, when they
populate treetops by the dozens, like little dark apples
while they wait for their mothers to gather salmon or
berries below. Riverside trees serve as an "ursine daycare,"
I read somewhere. Cute mental snapshot, but I'm a cub
waiting for this griz to go away, not come and collect me.

I look upward to see my treetop swaying in the
breeze like a carnival ride. It's maybe fifteen stories high,
a dwarf compared to surrounding lodgepole pines and
Sitka spruces, but those are less climber-friendly, like
Mussett said. The sturdy branches of my perch continue
to lead upward at well-spaced intervals, as if this speci-
men takes pride in training novices.

When the barbed-wire fence and cannery come into
view, my curiosity leads me higher, shaking but relieved

to be out of reach of Stud Griz, still using his dating app. Maybe ten storeys up, I find a secure nook where I can sit on a broad branch, lean back against the sturdy trunk, and enjoy an excellent view of the cannery. It looks as abandoned and lifeless as it should, but I know better. Before launching my drone on an exploratory, I pull out my binoculars and scan every inch of the place. Every graffitied wall, broken shingle, and rotting boardwalk plank. Every sagging window frame and pile of debris. After ten minutes of scanning, I'm bored.

Stud Griz has finished with the rubbing tree and is loping uphill. My pulse rises as I watch him pick up his pace close to the fence, well above the last cannery buildings. He's striding with a purpose now, almost like he's going to crash through the barbed wire. But wait. There's an opening, a short missing section of fencing. Clipped on purpose? I watch him gallop through it toward a small clearing and raise his snout to sniff.

Something ahead of him glints in the sun: something small and metal. Zooming in on the object with my binoculars, I draw in a breath. It's the size and shape of a steering wheel, but has steel teeth and a heavy chain attached to it. Please don't let it be a leg trap. That's a cruel way to catch any animal, sometimes snapping shut right to the bone.

Fumbling to bring my pack in front of me, I fish out my controller to capture whatever's about to happen. It's awkward launching Bug from my shaky seat, but soon he's in the air and hovering over the metal object and a barrel of garbage beside it. Garbage? It looks like there's food inside, on top, and spread all around the barrel, which is attached to a tree. Bear bait! Alarm bells go off in my head, as Stud Griz's humpy back and droopy buttocks make for the food. No way will I sit still while a healthy male bear steps into a leg trap set by bear-baiting poachers. I realize I want to prevent this disaster-in-motion more than I want to document it. So I turn my little guy right into Stud Griz's face and circle his head, annoying him like a mechanical bee.

It distracts him from his purpose, making him swat at the drone and back away from the trap. Yes! Keeping my heroic drone just out of reach of those killer paws, I attempt to lead him away from the clearing, away from the trap, which is ready to spring and cut deeply into the golden fur of his sturdy legs.

What I don't expect is a horde of mini-drones to fly out from one of the cannery buildings and beeline for Bug. Where did they come from? I've heard of federal prisons, industrial business sites, and airports keeping fleets of small drones on standby to swarm recreational drones that wander too close. There's good reason: Drones have been known to deliver cellphones, information, drugs, and guns to inmates, which is why prison guards have started using this kind of defence. And thieves sometimes use drones to spy on a building's security guards, in order to better time a robbery. Commercial properties are simply trying to protect their interests. But the interests of this particular operation are off-the-charts nasty.

Whatever I expected today, it certainly wasn't to en-counter a formation of enemy drones. Like a biblical drove of insects all but darkening the sky — well, okay, I see about fifty of them, anyway — such swarms typically drive off would-be intruders through intimidation and physical chase-dodge-and-bluff tactics. Worse, they'll follow the intruder home.

Bug's got the least stamina of my fleet. He can fly twenty minutes max. With only ten minutes left in him right now, and nothing to show on his camera but a glinting metal object and a hungry bear, my store-bought drone needs to either shake off the nasties on his tail or land anywhere but where he started, at the foot of this tree. Half-choked, I realize I need him to lead the swarm on a wild-goose chase, then sacrifice himself to a higher cause — in other words, drop out of the sky when he runs out of juice, somewhere far away from me. Otherwise, their drones will follow Bug straight to me.

He follows my reluctant orders to lift up and away toward Campsite 78. Let my rival drone operator think I'm tenting up there. There's a ghost of a chance I can retrieve the drone later. For now, he needs to valiantly keep his two siblings and me safe. Bug stays in the game most of the way up the mountainside, but goes down in a thicket of salal somewhere just short of the campsite, leaving me devastated, guilty, pissed off at his pursuers, and with little hope I'll ever see him again.

Meanwhile, in the little clearing above the cannery, the grizzly is bellowing in pain, probably from a deep wound in his leg after stepping into the trap despite my drone's efforts. A bearded man appears, running up from the cannery, carrying a large-calibre rifle. Oakley Logan. He's on his own because I disabled his brother's boat, I'm guessing. So that means he was operating the drones? *A man of many talents*, I think bitterly: My father's former classmate and my granddad's hunting buddy is skilled at kidnapping, milking, killing, and chopping up bears. I close my eyes and cover my ears.

In the poachers' warped minds, Stud Griz is too big to wrestle into a milking stall, and therefore needs to be shot and butchered for his valuable bits. For his paws, skull, hide, and gallbladder. I dare not launch Butterfly to film it happening, and lose my best spy as a result. There's Skyliner, but his forte is flying at night or inside dark buildings. I may yet need him for those tasks.

Even if I could film what's coming, I'm sure I'd lose my stomach contents. And yet, while Oakley's busy, this is my chance to sneak into the unguarded cannery and free Hank.

CHAPTER EIGHTEEN

THE MINUTE MY feet land on firm ground beneath the fir, I sprint downhill toward the bay, ducking under trees for cover from drone detection. Not that Oakley can dissect a bear and operate Yellow Drone at the same time, right? I roll under the barbed-wire fence near where it ends at the water — the place my binoculars saw the camouflage motorboat enter under the dock during the school trip.

Wading between the pilings through the salt water — with floating bits of wood and an occasional dead fish bumping against my legs — I pull out my headlamp. Under the dock, I spot a ramp-and-trap-door entry into the warehouse. Though the trap door has a padlock, it doesn't take me long to break it using the bolt cutters I liberated from Granddad's part of the garage.

I lift the trap door slowly and find myself in the giant warehouse, which smells as rotten as New York City during a summer garbage strike. Stacks of unused cans still await the fresh salmon that processors years ago would have packed, probably for a back-breaking number of hours per day. Now, the unused tins sit in corners like a museum display.

Kneeling on the worn planks, I pause to listen, but hear only the lapping of waves beneath me, the whistle of the wind blowing along the roofline, and chirps from birds nesting in the eaves. Thanks to chinks in the wall, some missing planks, and the glassless window frames, it's light enough for Butterfly to travel ahead of me, so I launch her and tiptoe a safe distance behind, turning her every which way on her travels to ensure there are no traps.

She passes from the warehouse to a far corridor, flitting between half-rotted walls and under corrugated metal roofing so aged and rusty that I'm extra careful to keep her from touching it. A roosting pigeon dives, but I skillfully steer Butterfly away.

When she reaches a closed door at the end of the hallway, I ease her down to rest on the doorstep and approach as silently as possible. Could this be the office? I pick up Butterfly and turn the doorknob. Not locked. The door hinges squeak just a little as I push it open an inch or two. The stench hits me first, enough to make me gag. Oily sweat, animal excrement, and the foul whiff of bodily infections only a vet could identify. Then I hear the sound of grunting and whining from a dark corner.

Through the door crack, I decide I am indeed viewing the room with the desk and cages I saw through my goggles while on the precipice with Min-jun and Cole. It has the same plastic-covered hole in the roof, the plywood desk with a chair and tray of medical equipment, and two coolers. And yes, the shelf of cages holding captive figures.

Entering the low-ceilinged room, the first thing I do is push up a corner of the plastic sheet over the roof hole and lift Butterfly onto the tin roof. She's now out of sight, but still under my control. Quickly, I stash the remote in my backpack.

Flicking on my headlamp and pinching my nostrils shut, I approach the dank, scary, putrid-smelling shelf, noting that the cages are locked, complicating my rescue of their occupants but also preventing them from springing out and mauling me. Nor are my lightweight bolt cutters going to get anywhere on the thick steel bars.

Choked at this setback, I draw nearer, like an onlooker at an accident scene. Small bears are moaning in the cages, banging their heads against the bars, chewing on their own paws.

I count: seven cages, four young bears. And there's Hank! He still has the cast on his paw. The other three bears look older than him. They're all in distressing states of deteriorating health, and all too large for the cages. They look starved and dehydrated, with missing teeth, stringy muscles, bald patches, and swollen limbs. Hairy arms and feet full of sores stick out from between the bars.

Trays beneath the cages catch their urine and feces — and haven't been emptied for a long time. Each bear has a plastic catheter stuck in its abdomen, most with rotting sores surrounding the wound. And there, as I noticed before, are the syringes, forceps, scalpels, and tubing sitting on the desktop beside the cages, as well as the muzzles hanging from hooks on the wall.

I have to turn away to keep from vomiting, crying, and screaming all at the same time. What kind of inhuman being could do this to any animal?

Hank is in a middle cage. I reach over to touch his limp, outstretched paw, my entire body contracting with sobs. He looks at me with hurt, glazed eyes. Though I know it's way too heavy, I want to lift his cage and run with it down the corridor, back through the warehouse, down through the trap door, and all the way back to my base. But every cage is locked and super heavy, and it may be only seconds before Oakley reappears or Orion chugs to the site with a borrowed boat or motor. In fact, who knows whether more than the two of them are in on this operation? Besides, they're probably on high alert, having swarmed one of my drones a short while ago.

I search the desk and shelves frantically, looking for cage keys or Yellow Drone. I notice that the shelf holding the cages doesn't quite meet the warped wall behind it. There's a gap, a dark space surely full of poisonous spiders, rats, and spilled bear excrement. *Oh, stop thinking the worst, Ray.* When the bears start to whimper in response to footsteps moving down the corridor, I quickly judge it's not large enough to hide me, but I can hide under the desk. I push my backpack, which is too big to fit under the desk with me, into the spider hole and crawl under the desk, then pull the chair in front of me, all but wetting myself in the process.

"Was a messy job but you should see the size of the claws," Oakley is saying in a lighthearted tone as he kicks the door open and strides through it. "What d'ya mean ya can't make it? I'm not doin' a double shift, ya lunk."

So he's talking on a cellphone. Lucky for him there's good enough reception here.

"The outboard? What the hell? That's worth, like, nothing! Why'd anyone bother? Well, borrow or steal one and get your ass over 'ere 'fore Chee shows up."

Chee? Who's *that*?

"I don't care! Just do it, numbnuts!"

There's a little bleep, like he's hung up on his brother.

"Okay, creatures," he says, and I hear the jingling of keys. "It's not my turn, but you reekin' douchebags are in for suppertime, followed by milkin' hour. While my idiot brother sits on his ass."

It seems talking to animals isn't just a vet thing.

I'm all but holding my breath as I sit crunched up under the desk. Then I hear a sound more terrifying than the bears' crying: the skittering of dog claws along the corridor. Chief comes bolting in, barking joyfully, like he knows it's feeding time for him as well. And it takes the Doberman all of a split second to stick his large black nose under the chair and into my face and yelp excitedly at discovering my cringing, sweating, shaking body.

I have a can of bear spray on my belt, but hell will freeze over before I ever use it on an innocent dog.

Though bred to take down strangers, Chief doesn't sink his teeth into me. I'm lucky. Then again, it's not pure luck. He knows me. His tail is wagging enough to almost trip a shocked Oakley.

I use that second to shove the chair into Chief's and Oakley's legs, leap out of my cubby, and sprint toward the door. But Oakley's long arm grabs me by the neck of my sweater, as Chief leaps about us.

Even in nice neighbourhoods of New York City, you don't grow up without learning some defence tactics for situations like this, and my knee goes straight for Oakley's balls.

"Arghhh!" He doubles over in agony.

By then I'm out the door and putting boot tread to rotting planks down the dark corridor and into the warehouse. I'm nearly to the trap door when some kind of noose drops over my head and yanks me to the ground, strangling me. I try to scream but can't. My hands grab for my neck but the noose tightens, forcing me to lie still and silent. Next thing I know, Chief is licking my face.

"You little prick. How'd ya get in 'ere? Thought you'd explore and then jist saunter out? You're dead, little McLellan. Not going nowhere now."

I'm struggling to breathe. Is he going to kill me? How can he afford not to, now that I know what I know?

"This 'ere's called a capture pole," he boasts, holding the end of the pole over me with his trigger finger on the spring-loaded wire that tightens the noose cable. "Great

for nabbin' cubs. Never used it on a brainless varmint
'fore. Hey, Chief, lay off. What kinda guard dog're you,
slobberin' over 'im like that?"

I say nothing, just kick my ankles as a signal of distress and point my fingers at the plastic-coated cable
against my Adam's apple.

"Aha, we wanna breathe, do we? Well, I can loosen
it if ya stand up and start marchin' back to where I
found ya."

I nod, a gurgling sound emerging as he returns some
of my airway to me.

Like a fish on the end of a pole, I rise. He grabs the
bear spray off my belt, then frisks me and takes away
my phone and bolt cutters. Fine. At least he missed the
small bag of sedatives, and he doesn't know about the
stowed backpack.

Guided by the choke ring, I move ahead of him down
the corridor, Chief's tail batting against my knees. I've
stuck one little finger under the noose in a vain attempt
to save myself if he tightens it again. The bruise-ring
that the capture pole has created smarts. In the office,
Oakley leaves the door open behind us.

"Lie down," he orders, and I'm confused till I see
Chief drop obediently to the floor.

Then, one hand still firm on the capture pole, he pulls
a ring of keys out of his jeans pocket, opens the largest
empty cage, and delivers a swift kick to my butt.

"No!" I shout with my recovered breath, but as he lifts
the noose off me, I feel the rifle barrel resting against
my back.

"Get in, now!" he shouts.

The cage he's pushing me into is a poor fit for my frame. My neck is bent, my legs crossed, and I'm cramping up already. But he's not going to shoot me if he's putting me in a cage, right?

The lock clicks, and his angry, glinting eyes meet mine. "We'll decide later what ta do," he mutters. He tosses the keys in the top desk drawer, slams it shut, and storms out of the room even as his fingers are tapping his phone.

Who's "we"? I wonder ominously. I glance sideways at my ursine companions and feel every nerve ending of their pain. The bars don't allow any of us to move our bodies more than an inch in any direction.

Judging from the sunlight moving across the skylight, I'm there for hours — most of the day. Despite the discomfort, the reek, and the moans and shuffling of the bears, I somehow manage to doze off a few times. When I wake and notice the sunlight is fading to dusk, desperation jerks me to full attention. Slowly, an idea forms, one I wish I'd thought of hours before.

I find that with some wriggling, I can fit my arm between the bars at the back of the cage and lower my fingers to a loop on the backpack I tossed down the spider hole. I fumble in it for my remote controller, then gaze up to where Butterfly sits on the roof beside the flapping, plastic-sheeted skylight. She's fully charged and can fly longer than her drone siblings. She should make it to Dorothy's in less than forty-five minutes.

"Fly away home," I whisper. "Please."

The stench and unhappiness of the bears beside me fade as I concentrate on lifting Butterfly off the roof and directing her down the cannery property slope, over the water, and across the bay. I'll slam her against Dorothy's garage door, and Dorothy will know something's up. She'll look at the film. She'll guess where I am. She'll get help. Please, Butterfly, make it to Dorothy's. Please, Dorothy, be there. I can't stand to think about her not being there, or her not getting what my drone's visit means: that I need help ASAP at the cannery.

I hear Oakley shouting on the phone somewhere in the warehouse but can't make out his words. Then I hear a louder shout, and Butterfly's camera picks up Yellow Drone in hot pursuit, though Butterfly is surely barely visible from the cannery by now. Oakley — unless there's another person involved — has spotted and is chasing her, but he doesn't seem to assume it's me at the controls. At least, he hasn't hotfooted it back here to check on me. How could it be me, a captive in a cage? In his mind, it's got to be whoever is hanging out at Campsite 78.

Yellow Drone may be a bigger, badder UAV, but it's not as manoeuvrable as my nymph. We feint and dodge one another as we fly, using up precious energy. We clear the bay and are over town now, zigzagging in crazy motion, would-be predator and prey. Yellow Drone, drunk on aggression, almost knocks against Butterfly once, but Butterfly manages to give it the slip. Still, my baby is going to lose her advantage any second. The fighting has sucked out too much of her battery power. She's not going to make it to Dorothy's unless her flight path returns to a straight line. That's what Yellow Drone is waiting for, I know it. My joystick dances like crazy as Yellow Drone seems to move in for the kill.

Just then, a swarm of mini-drones led by a larger one comes screaming toward both of us. This is how Butterfly is going to die? Ingloriously, only two blocks away from the Dawsons' garage? Incapable of tapping on Dorothy's door, or lowering herself into Dorothy's tender palms? Who's behind this bombardment, anyway? Orion in phone coordination with his brother?

The enemy formation zooms in on Yellow Drone, not Butterfly. The mini-drones scream through the air at it, whirl around it like a tornado, and force it to the ground. On her last dregs of battery power, Butterfly lands in a yard a few houses away from Dorothy's place. But, astonishingly, the leader of the mystery fleet detaches from that group and hovers over her protectively while its minions continue to harass Yellow Drone. Suddenly, I recognize the leader. It's Dorothy's custom-made cherry-red drone, the one Butterfly duelled with on our first meetup!

My view of the scene now cuts out. Butterfly goes to sleep there among the dewy blades of grass in an unknown backyard, guarded by her surprise angel. I'm unable to see what must be occurring next: Dorothy's pink running shoes leaping over the fence and scooping up Butterfly, while her crazy dad, general of the mini-drone squadron, captures Yellow Drone before Yellow Drone's operator can recover that pricey pursuer. Mr. Dawson, original creator and seller of Yellow Drone, taking repossession for its bad behaviour.

From within my cage, my chest fills with hope, and with pride in Dorothy, but the sound of heavy boots stomping down the corridor toward me makes my heart slam against my ribs again. I drop my controller and backpack down the spider hole as fast as I can.

CHAPTER NINETEEN

"MR. KIM!" I shout in relief as he bursts through the door. "Help me, please! Oakley Logan locked me in here. He might come back any minute. And these bears —"

I choke on my words as he glares at me from the centre of the room, hands on his hips. "How dare you come here! We try warn you. Mess your workshop, make bears come to your campsite. Your grandfather say you city kid big scared of bears. But you no listen to warnings and come here now. Is bad, bad." He wrings his hands and shakes his head, jowls flapping.

"Mr. Kim?" My stomach clenches into a tight ball.

"These bears have special medicine. Keep Min-jun healthy. Keep your grandfather alive."

"What? No, they don't! That's bull!"

My mind is flying tight corners around my memory. I once heard that *kimchee* is an insulting name for Koreans, so does that mean Mr. Kim is Chee? And he's working with the Logan brothers? I recall the day he stared at me when I set up an IV in the clinic and how casually he reached for a muzzle to put on the retriever. And the time I overheard Mr. Dawson and him arguing in the Dawsons' garage. Delivering dumplings? Maybe. And perhaps negotiating to buy more drones to guard the cannery property.

Does Min-jun know what his father is up to? I bet he didn't before that day he, Cole, and I were on the cliff's edge, when he had a seizure and smashed my camera. Min-jun saw something that upset him, but I don't know what. It stressed him out, brought on the seizure. But I doubt he ruined the camera on purpose, or even remembers doing it.

Min-jun said his dad had upped the dosage. Of bear bile, I now know.

So, his father has been giving him bear bile in some form — pills, tea, whatever — rather than prescription drugs, thinking it's preventing seizures.

"Who's the boss, you or the Logan brothers?" I ask Mr. Kim through gritted teeth, my palms wrapped around the bars of my cage.

"Oakley and Orion work for big boss in China. I help for medicine."

"The Logan brothers dropped salmon in our campsite by drone?"

"Yes," he says with a grim smile. "Steal boat motor?" he demands.

"Maybe," I toss back, no longer feeling guilty about that.

"But is okay that Orion late to extract, because we have you," Mr. Kim declares, eyes on the bears like he's impatient to collect his allotment of the bile. "Vet who can do IV."

I turn to look at Hank and his sad buddies, quivering in their overtight prison cells, infections leaking pus where a butcher of a person has pushed tubes into them.

"Hank's not even old enough to be a bile bear. They're supposed to be three and up. You're killing them," I spit out.

"No, I save Min-jun and your grandfather," he says calmly, confidently.

He pulls the ring of keys out of the desk drawer and unlocks my cage. I want to dash past him and escape, but his fingers rest on my bruised neck. He eyes the capture pole beside us. "Sorry, Ray."

We stare at each other, this Mr. Kim I don't know and me.

"Does Granddad know, or does he just drink your tea to be polite?"

"It help him."

Of course Granddad doesn't know. He had vowed to mount the head of the poacher who is out pillaging bears for their body parts and their cubs.

Oakley has moved into the room now, his grin revealing stained teeth. "New helper," he says in a pleased voice.

"First feed bears, then collect bile," Mr. Kim tells me. "Oakley train you."

I bite my lip, contemplating what will happen if I refuse.

"Someone will come find me. And arrest you guys," I say.

"No," says Mr. Kim, "you run away, your grandfather say. Too sad about Mommy go away. No one know where you are. Great Bear Rainforest is very big."

Very big. Twelve thousand square miles. More than thirty thousand square kilometres. And he's right. By Dad's and Granddad's reckoning, I could be anywhere, not to mention unwilling to be found. Will Dorothy clue in?

I decide my safest course is to play the game. "You're right, I'm a trained vet," I say defiantly. "And you're doing a rotten job on your percutaneous biliary drainage. The area around the catheters is vulnerable to infection. And bile can leak back into the abdomen, killing the bears. They'll live longer and produce more bile for you if I take over."

They stare at me like they've been struck dumb.

Making my voice meeker, I add, "I didn't know you were helping Granddad like this, or Min-jun."

"I'll train this varmint," Oakley says, squinting his eyes at Mr. Kim. "Dismissed, Chee."

Mr. Kim winces at the name, throws me a half-apologetic look, and hands the keys to Oakley, who tosses them back into the desk drawer. Mr. Kim turns toward the door obediently as Oakley settles into the office chair. "I see you later."

"Later," Oakley mumbles. Mr. Kim shuffles through the door and pads down the corridor.

"Still got your ugly ear," Oakley tries to razz me. "Thought a rich boy like you might git plastic surgery, make it all handsome agin."

"You think I don't remember that camping trip," I retort.

"I know ya don't. Your granddad says ya don't 'member a thing. Only reason I got asked along was 'cause he hated the idea of babysittin' ya by hisself. So it was the three of us, gone campin.'"

I squeeze my eyes shut. The scene is stored away in my brain somewhere. If only I could coax it out intact. I reopen them and stare hard at Oakley, trying to imagine him without the beard. That's when the black and white film starts playing again, slowly at first, then faster …

I'm alone in Granddad's big canvas tent. I've awakened in the middle of the night, shivering. Something is outside the tent, sniffing, grunting, moving around. I slip deeper into my sleeping bag and whimper, "Granddad? Mr. Logan?"

Then I hear them, snoring. Outside the tent. I'm alone and it's very dark. Panic grips me. But I bite my tongue and move, very slowly, toward the tent flap. I peek out and scan the campsite. The campfire has gone very, very low. It's hardly burning at all anymore. An empty whiskey bottle sits between my two adult guardians, Granddad asleep in his camping chair, an open bag of wieners within reach. Mr. Logan is slumped against a large log closer to the tent.

A monster-sized grizzly is standing erect on the other side of the campfire, sniffing. My heart pounds so hard I nearly fall over backwards. The bear lowers its body, lumbers toward the package of meat, and places a paw on it, just feet from Granddad. In fact, it seems entirely unconcerned about the sleeping humans. I hold my breath, terror ripping through me. *Don't wake up, Granddad. Stay sleeping, Mr. Logan. Don't anyone move till it's gone.*

"Hey!" the young and unbearded Oakley shouts, sitting up suddenly. He scrambles backwards toward the tent on elbows and buttocks, frantically trying to find his gun in the dark.

"Daniel!" he calls in a choked voice as the bear looms over Granddad, his takeout meal in hand.

The bear's going to kill Granddad now, maybe Mr. Logan, too. The men are too close, not even a 747 wingspan away from the surprised animal. Even at age five, I know the 747 rule.

I dash out of the tent, pick up a rock, and toss it straight at the bear, hitting its chest. Then, keeping the campfire between us, I pick up a metal-pronged marshmallow roasting stick from the fire and shake it at our camp visitor, distracting it away from Granddad. In my mind, I'm an armoured knight with a sword, and the dying campfire is a foolproof shield the bear can't cross.

"Get away!" I scream. "Leave us alone!"

The bear widens its eyes to a scary yellow, flattens its ears, and barrels toward me. I scream loud enough to wake up every bird and animal in the forest as the grizzly swats the left side of my head, sending me flying. I land hard on packed dirt and rocks, the world spinning, and wait for the grizzly's body to crush me, the claws to puncture my small frame, the teeth to tear off my scalp. By then, Granddad and Mr. Logan are up and shouting, spraying stuff that drifts down to me and stings my eyes. I squeeze my lids shut tightly, waiting for death. My heart's pounding too hard to hear anything after that. But I feel the ground rumble as the grizzly turns and gallops off.

It was capable of killing us all but was more interested in hot dogs that night. Thank God.

Granddad picks me up gently, examines my head, and applies pressure on the ear wound with a clean cloth. When it stops bleeding, he washes it with soap and water, then puts a dab of cool antiseptic cream on it from his first-aid pack. All that as Oakley Logan now stands guard with a gun.

"Yer a brave and lucky tyke," Granddad's saying, head shaking, a warmth in his voice that melts the edges of my icy fear. "A crazy eejit to be sure, without a speck of outdoors sense in you yet. If you'd left him be, he'd have moved on, grandson. Didn't need yer suicidal heroics. It's all yer fault he got in a flap, Ray. But ..."

I don't remember anything after the "yer fault," a phrase he repeated endlessly as they drove me through the darkness to the Bella Coola Hospital. Maybe he thought drumming that into me would protect him from my parents' wrath over Oakley and him falling asleep with meat beside them while on child-care duty.

I don't remember my parents' reaction or anything about what the doctors did for my damaged ear. I blocked it all out, somehow, along with the bear attack itself — until just now. Mostly what stays is that moment before it all happened: the terror of waking up alone in the tent and knowing something was wrong. And the moment of waiting for the bear to finish me off.

No wonder I'm afraid of being alone in the woods and don't have confidence in my so-called outdoors sense.

Technically, it was indeed my fault the bear got angry. And that sense of guilt may be why I've always refused Mom's offers of plastic surgery to repair my ear. And because I'm as stubborn as she is, I made sure she couldn't make me. Or maybe it's just down to McLellan stubbornness, the same stubbornness that set Granddad against me from that day. "Yer fault. No speck of outdoors sense in you." A refrain he has repeated all my life, no doubt because he was caught napping in a whiskey stupor and almost witnessed my death as a result. Both he and I conveniently forgot one small fact: I was only five years old.

"That bear could have killed all of us," I say now to Oakley. "It wasn't my fault. It was all about you and Granddad not returning the wieners to the strung-up food bag. And you waking up and yelling at the wrong time."

Oakley's neck goes patchy as he turns to me. "So ya do 'member somethin'. But ya don't throw rocks at a bear, son."

"And you don't get drunk and fall asleep in bear country with meat next to you and a campfire going out."

"You win," he mutters. "It's true you maybe saved my hide, me wakin' up in an untimely fashion. Though I still think that beast took off 'cause he knew you was jist a cub. And he didn't like the bear spray. As for falling asleep on the job, your granddad got in major trouble from your parents for 't."

"I don't remember that," I say, trying to picture Granddad cowering in front of my parents.

Oakley chuckles. "He's a curmudgeon, your granddad. Ornery as they come. It's what keeps him alive, 'long with the bile tea."

So Oakley buys into the whole bile-as-medicine theory? With effort, I hold my tongue. Somehow I need to get out of this place alive. How? Get Oakley on my side?

CHAPTER TWENTY

MY SMILE DISAPPEARS. "Dad said you always wanted to be a vet."

"Yeah." He lifts his head and directs his gaze at the vet kit.

"How often do you collect bile from the bears?"

"Twice a day. Is quick 'n easy, even if they howl like bastards. Only hard part is settin' up new bears that come in."

"You mean having to cut a hole through their chests into the gallbladder to fit the permanent catheter?" I wince to even say it.

"Smart boy. Yup. Then we use a twelve-centimetre needle to git the bile flowin' through the tube."

I swallow my own bile down and avert my eyes from Hank.

"What about bears too big to, um, set up? You bait and kill them to cut their gallbladders out? How do you know what to use for bait?"

He grins proudly. "Sometimes we use a road-killed deer or dead beaver. But fruit cover'd in brown sugar works real good. So does vanilla extract!" He chuckles like a proud chef.

"Are you the drone operator, too?" I can't believe he's sharing like this. Does it mean he's going to off me?

He grins. "We paid Mr. Dawson to outfit 'n train me. It's fun, ain't it, squirt?"

"Total fun," I agree.

"Someone campin' up top been at it today. One of your buddies?"

"Not that I know of. Hey, can I really help with the next collection?" It's the last thing in the entire universe I want to do, but I'm forming an escape plan.

He shrugs. "Why not, vet kid?"

"So, when's that? And we're free till then?"

"Ten minutes. And *I'm* free till then. You're in a cage, asshole."

"Right. Well, ten minutes to kill, then," I say casually, instantly regretting my choice of words. I watch as Oakley produces a dish and can opener from the desk, opens a can of dogfood, and serves it to Chief, who chows it down happily.

Oakley watches him, looking bored, while sipping from a water bottle. A beeper on his watch goes off ten minutes later. "Milkin' time!" he announces, lifting the keys out of the desk drawer with a jingle and letting me out. I stretch in relief. Oakley reaches down beside the desk for one of the coolers. He lifts out some unpalatable-looking food and slops it into a bowl, then opens up Hank's cage.

My hands dart in to encircle the orphan, and I manage to carry all one hundred–plus pounds of him to the office chair, where I place him on my lap. Oakley hands me the bowl of food and I lift it to Hank's mouth. Oatmeal and honey. He just lies there limply. Oakley passes me a spoon and I try coaxing Hank like he's a baby in a high chair. His pink mouth opens, and my heart weeps as he licks the spoon weakly, eyes unfocused on my face. He's definitely not the healthy, happy, trusting orphan who slurped mashed fruit out of a bowl such a short time ago.

"Do you have local anesthetic, antibiotics, antiseptic, and sutures or staples to close some of their wounds with?" I ask Oakley.

He shrugs and points to the veterinary first-aid kit case. It's basic, the kind sold over the internet. I go through it and sigh.

Next, Oakley clamps a muzzle on Hank. While his back is turned preparing the needle, I reach into my pocket and slip the sedatives I snatched from my parents' clinic into my palm, then crush them on the desk with the forceps and funnel them into my captor's water bottle. I've already judged the man's weight, and I'm administering the correct dose, more or less.

Oakley hands me the syringe and barks directions at me that I don't need and can't stomach.

What I do next I will not describe. Except to say that Hank screeches like he is being tortured all during the procedure. They are the cries of a ghoul in everlasting pain. No wonder this place is rumoured to be haunted. Oakley just stands and watches, sipping from his water bottle.

As I finish the bile extraction, Oakley grabs Hank from my arms and returns him roughly to his cage, fetching the next prisoner. This one's in worse shape, has clearly been here longer. His catheter insertion was a botch of a job, and his teeth are all but gone, probably from trying to bite his way through the steel bars. Unlike Hank, he has totally lost the will to eat.

"Faster," Oakley orders, as I work my way through the bears, feeding and then milking them, all the while breathing through my mouth to avoid taking in the stench of their festering sores.

Finally, I turn to the recaged grizzlies I've just tortured against my will and against the veterinarian's oath.

"Can I stay out of my cage now?" I ask, hands shaking, guilt suffocating me.

"Not likely, nut-kicker," Oakley says, pushing me toward my cage, both the capture pole and the rifle within reach in case I try anything. I climb back in and sigh as he clicks the door shut on my chamber, locks it, and returns the keys to the desk drawer once again.

It takes almost an hour for him to doze off. During that time, I watch the light through the flapping plastic on the roof fade and then darken. It's nighttime, and dead silent except for the disturbed breathing and movements of the cubs. I poke my arm through the rear bars and fish up my backpack again. Chief stirs and watches me.

"Here boy," I say, stuffing what remains of the sedatives from the vet clinic into half of the ham sandwich I brought and extending my arm through the front bars to offer the treat to him. He snaps it up so quickly I momentarily fear losing my fingers. I stuff the undrugged portion of the sandwich into my mouth and begin the wait for the Doberman to hit Dreamland.

Now I reach into the backpack for my last remaining drone. It's too large to slide into the cage with me, but I don't need to. I need only the controller and my goggles.

"Okay, Skyliner," I say, holding my precious prize in my palm outside the bars. "My skill, your hook, and we're out of here, with all the photographic evidence we need."

The dog stirs and lifts his head once as the drone starts up, then settles into a deep sleep. Hands on the controller, I direct my UAV to hover over the desk, then twist and turn him until he has lowered his hook through the drawer handle.

Accelerating him back toward me, I hold my breath as he pulls the drawer open, just a little, not enough to knock against the office chair and its deeply sleeping inhabitant. Now I have to wriggle Skyliner to get the hook out of the desk handle, back him up, and then have a try at snagging the ring of keys in the drawer.

"Don't drop them on the dog or Oakley," I whisper.

Yes! Like a well-trained retriever, Skyliner helicopters back over to me with keys dangling beneath his tummy. He hovers obediently outside the cage till I can reach through and grab them. "Good boy," I say. With both hands stuck out of the bars like robot arms, I tuck the drone back into my backpack.

I listen carefully for a few minutes before finding the key that opens my cage. There's no sound but the rasping bears, snoring man, and wheezing Doberman. I wish I could sedate the bears to ease their pain, but I didn't bring enough medication.

Just as I free myself, Oakley's phone buzzes. I whip it away from his shirt pocket and dash into the hall. No screen lock on his phone, and there's a text from Mr. Kim: *Anderson on way. Police have Orion. Make all cub and cage go away?*

Lucky the call didn't wake Oakley up. I reply *ok*, pocket the phone, and use Skyliner to record the room, cages, pitiful bears, and vet equipment. I do it again with Oakley's phone as a backup. My heart goes heavy as I film the cubs. I can't free all of them and make a quick getaway. Even Hank would be a dangerous burden. "I'll be back," I promise in a whisper. Finally, I step over Chief, shrug on my backpack, and tiptoe down the hallway.

I send Skyliner flitting along the corridor ahead to make sure I'm not going to walk into Mr. Kim. So he thinks he's going to ditch the evidence for the Logan brothers, does he? As soon as I'm out of here, I'll be phoning 911 on the stolen phone. In the big, echoing warehouse, I train my headlamp on the rotted floorboards beneath my feet to make sure I don't fall through.

When I'm under the building's collapsed roof section, I fly Skyliner up into the night to survey the grounds. "Find Mr. Kim," I whisper. The UAV spots a weak light coming from the tiny clearing up the hill, the place where Stud Griz met his fate.

"Okay, spy, go film him," I tell my night drone, and he's off, high enough in the dark sky that Mr. Kim won't easily see or hear him. Excited to experience Skyliner's night-vision capabilities, I let him hover high above the site and record what the man is up to: He's using a pole with a hook on the end to pull dark items out of a pit only feet from the leg traps and bear bait. As I zoom in, my heart drops. Bear claws. Dozens of them. He's fishing them out of a deep, dark hole and loading them into a large backpack. At nine hundred dollars per claw (and five claws per paw), they must be worth a fortune. But my stomach turns over to think what was involved in collecting them.

"Bastard," I say under my breath, as Skyliner collects the scene on his memory card.

Okay, I've now recorded the caged bears, the office, the hidden stash of claws, and the two men. Now I have to go hide with Skyliner till daybreak. But my last glimpse of what I'm filming chokes off my breath: Mr. Kim looking straight up into Skyliner's eye and lifting his pole.

Just as I press the return-home button, my view goes all crazy, like Skyliner is tumbling through the air. Then the picture on my goggles goes dead.

No! Mr. Kim must have thrown his pole up like a spear and whacked my prince, and now Skyliner is lying wounded somewhere in that disgusting clearing, in serious danger. But no way is Mr. Kim getting his filthy hands on my genius! I sprint to the trap door, yank it open, and splash into the ankle-deep water. Then I hightail it up the hill.

CHAPTER TWENTY-ONE

WITH MY HEADLAMP switched off, I'm navigating by weak starlight, tripping and stumbling over the rough ground, trying not to fall face first onto rusty nails, sharp metal roofing pieces, and other rubble. But picturing Skyliner lying on his belly, prey for a man determined to bludgeon him to death, puts fire in my calves.

I burst into the clearing just as Mr. Kim raises a rock over my drone, and I leap forward to tackle him. He's twice my size, but I have adrenalin coursing through every vein, and enough of a surprise factor to knock him over. I'm on top of Mr. Kim, trying to pin down his arms, then he's on top of me, punching me in the face.

Remembering the rules for surviving a bear attack, I cover my head and neck with locked hands.

"How you get out of cage? Where Oakley?" Mr. Kim is shouting in a panicked voice.

I have no idea if there are gangs in the Korea he grew up in, but I put all my city-boy fight into keeping him away from Skyliner, and we roll on the damp grass this way and that, once right into the pile of mushy bear bait — which turns out to be stinky fish — scattered at the foot of the barrel.

Like mud wrestlers, we're now covered in the most foul-smelling crap my nostrils have ever inhaled. He's getting the better of me, but I'm still in the fight. I have nothing personal against my neighbour, and can't believe we're even tussling, but I'm like a grizzly mom within feet of her threatened cub.

Suddenly I'm aware we're slipping downhill. We're tumbling toward the open leg traps! With all the strength left in me, I free a hand to clutch a rock and toss it straight at the nearest iron circle.

Snap! Its toothy jaws grip the rock instead of our legs and startles us into a microsecond's pause. I use that opportunity to spring up and leap toward Skyliner. Mr. Kim's hands close over my ankles just as my fingers clutch Skyliner's belly hook. In the moment before my foe can yank me back to a final match, I lift and toss my favourite child into the bear-claw pit. Soft fur will be her landing spot, I hope.

There's a strong, painful wrench on my ankles, and my bruised body gets dragged back to Mr. Kim's meaty grip. I come to rest in the mud with my neck on top of an uncomfortable, smelly lump. Mr. Kim's hands grip my throat, and his knees are crushing my thighs. As he raises a fist for a punch, I grab whatever is behind my neck and swipe him with it.

"Arghhh!" he cries, and his fist just misses my face. I turn back in time to see I've scraped one of his ears with the claws of a bear paw.

"Dad!" comes an agitated voice out of the darkness.

We both freeze. There's only the sound of windblown trees and footsteps coming up the hill beneath us.

"Min-jun?" Mr. Kim says.

"Ray!" shouts a familiar voice behind him.

"Dad!" I cry in astonishment.

I'm still braced for a lights-out hit, and I'm shaking all over. How did Min-jun and Dad get here in the middle of the night? What made them come? And how'd they find us in this pitch-black mini-clearing?

Dad charges at Mr. Kim and tackles him. I roll free. Mr. Kim lies still, as if defeated. Four more faces come into view behind Min-jun and Dad: Dorothy, her father, Officer Anderson, and a uniformed cop. What? *Butterfly! You did it!*

Officer Anderson moves quickly to put plastic hand restraints on Mr. Kim. Dad stands and rushes over and places his arms around me. My shaking calms slightly as I melt into his warm body.

Officer Anderson turns to me. "Dorothy figured you were trying to signal her with your drone, so she called Min-jun, who confirmed you were probably here at the cannery. Then she called your father and me," he tells me. "I just got back today from a week's vacation, so

I didn't get your earlier messages. Mr. Dawson came along to fly a night-vision drone across the property so we could find you."

I release Dad and slowly move toward Dorothy. We embrace, and intense happiness chases away my fear and pain. Then I nod politely to her father, still trying to catch my breath.

"Was it you who deployed the mini-drones to run off the one chasing my spy UAV?" I ask him.

"Dorothy and I did it together. We're a team," he says proudly.

"Always ready to help civilians in distress," Dorothy says with a wink.

"Aye aye," I reply. "Oakley's inside the warehouse," I tell Officer Anderson. "Probably still sleeping."

"What?" Mr. Kim erupts. "He sleep while I do dirty work for him?"

"Sedated with vet medicine, along with Chief," I inform the poacher accomplice. His eyes widen.

I turn on slightly shaky legs and survey Min-jun, who is staring at the spilled backpack of bear claws, the bear-bait barrel, and the rock-sprung leg trap, his shoulders slumped. "Thanks, bro," I say. He nods without looking at me. He won't look at his dad. I can feel his pain.

I move up the rise to the bear-claw stash and retrieve Mr. Kim's stick to pull out Skyliner. Gently, I give my drone a full inspection. He seems to have survived the fall intact.

"Was all for you," Mr. Kim says to his son, and then breaks into rapid-fire Korean, presumably all about what he believes bear bile can do.

"We should've listened to Mom and done Western medicine," Min-jun says, shaking his head and backing away, while Officer Anderson and the cop help Mr. Kim to his feet and lead us all toward the warehouse.

There, Officer Anderson claps restraints on an astonished and dopey Oakley, then lets my father and me treat Mr. Kim's face gashes with the first-aid kit. The rest of the group stares, hands to their mouths, at the row of caged cubs. Dorothy makes little gagging sounds but manages to hold down her disgust.

"They put me in that cage," I say, indicating the empty one. "They didn't know I had my drone hidden in a gap behind the shelf. I used its hook to open the drawer and fetch the keys. It also has night-vision capabilities that allowed me to find Mr. Kim. He'd sent a text message to Oakley after Oakley fell asleep, about getting rid of everything." I move protectively toward Hank's cage. "As in eliminating the bears," I emphasize.

"Hey!" Oakley objects as I hand his phone to Officer Anderson. Then I get my phone, bear spray, and bolt cutters off him.

Hearing trap-door hinges squeak in the warehouse space down the hall, we move toward it. Even though I'm surrounded by other people, I'm a little alarmed. Two bodies scramble up onto the warehouse floorboards: more police officers.

In their powerful flashlight beams, Dad sees my face clearly for the first time. "Ray," he says, drawing me to him again and gently touching the bruises and welts on my neck and face. "You're hurt!"

"I'm good," I reply, leaning into his warm hands on my shoulder.

"Your mother never made it past Vancouver," he says in a rush. "I told her you'd run away and she is on her way home — for good. She said she realized before the plane landed that she was making a mistake and she's sorry. Very sorry." He takes a deep breath to hide a tremble in his voice. "So, we have some bears to transfer to the clinic right now. Looks like some are in critical condition."

"Hank's in horrible pain, but I didn't have enough medicine to sedate the bears and —"

"Shhh," Dad says. "There will be time for stories later. Patients first."

CHAPTER TWENTY-TWO

FIFTEEN MEMBERS OF the Bella Coola High School Outdoors Club are standing soberly in the lashing rain at Campsite 78, forming a long horizontal line, facing forward. Each of us holds a stick. We move two steps, four steps, keeping our line even. Our sticks sweep back and forth, our eyes glued on the thick undergrowth through which we're making our way. I'm between Dorothy and Min-jun. Chief is prancing around near me. He's become my dog since the Logan brothers went off to prison, and we've become best buddies.

"Outdoors Club!" Cole shouts. He's up front, facing us. "As we've discussed, this is how search-and-rescue teams find people missing in the backcountry. They proceed in a row, slowly, eyes trained on the ground. Today, we're looking for a 250-millimetre, one-pound graphite drone with four propellers. A quadcopter that sacrificed itself to save one of our valued members, as well as the bears in our forest. Whether or not we find it, we can say we tried. And we'll learn valuable wilderness search-and-rescue techniques at the same time."

He winks at me, turns, and begins moving his stick back and forth in front of him, like he's operating a metal detector in a field of gold pieces.

We search for an hour. I grow frustrated and disappointed, though I keep my chin up and feel grateful for the help. We get chilled and soaked, even in our best rain gear. We don't find my drone, but I whisper "Thanks, Bug," as we head back to the minibus. Talking to drones? Yeah, that's a thing with droners. Or at least, with me.

The best part is when we reach the minibus and get served hot drinks by our teacher Mr. Mussett and his wife, along with kimchee mandu, fresh made by Min-jun.

Min-jun, who has handed over club presidency to Cole, has been kind of quiet since the Logan brothers were taken away and his father was sentenced to some time — though less than originally expected, since his dad fully cooperated with police and testified against the main players.

I visit Min-jun regularly, bringing him mistletoe tea I ordered online, since it's supposed to help his condition. Who knows, but it's the thought that counts, just like between Mr. Kim and my granddad. "Might get you a girlfriend even if it doesn't help," I kid him.

"Things are tough at home," Min-jun has confessed to me, "with my mom and me having to handle the café all by ourselves. We appreciate it when you help out." He continued with chin down. "We miss my dad, though it won't be long now. He was only trying to help me, you know. He hated the killing stuff the Logan brothers were up to. And how they bossed him around."

"I know. How's your health?" I asked him.

"Better since my mom took me back to our Bella Coola doctor. He prescribed me new stuff without any side effects. So I'm all good, it seems like."

Min-jun also swore to me that he doesn't remember what he saw when he was wearing my goggles, and that he has no memory of smashing my drone camera. "So sorry," he said to me, stricken at the info. "But I knew you were obsessed with the cannery. I guessed it was about Hank, so that's what I told Dorothy when she called. And decided I had to go with her."

Dorothy is sitting beside me on a mossy log near the minibus, her shoulder touching mine, a plate of dumplings on her lap. "Are you really top chef at your café now?" she asks Min-jun.

"Yes," he says quietly with a small smile. "My mom and I are running it till Dad … gets out."

"Well, if this is your secret recipe, we're all going to be there every day after school," Cole's new gymnastics-star girlfriend declares, and everyone murmurs agreement.

I squeeze Dorothy's hand, and she squeezes mine back. "You look good in your new hipster flannel shirt and cowboy hat under that designer rain poncho," she says, giggling a little.

"Thanks. I picked a colour that would match my beret if I ever go back to wearing it," I tease.

She lifts her hand and touches my left ear. "So, it wasn't a bike accident, or a girl who got carried away while kissing it, or a mountain lion bite, or a New York City gang brand, or frostbite."

"No," I say. "It was a grizzly cuffing me for pointing a marshmallow stick at it."

Everyone around us bursts into laughter. "Best one yet!" someone says gleefully.

"Actually," I tell them soberly, "that's the real story."

"I believe you," Dorothy says, a serious look in her chestnut eyes. "Only because you were five."

"I was five. And my damaged ear is actually an advantage, because it buzzes when grizzly bears are near."

The others look startled and exchange comments about this. "Cool," says one girl. "I'm sticking near you on hikes."

"Ahem," says Cole, grabbing our attention. "So, as your new prez, I have an announcement. We're going to have a special field trip next weekend if it's not raining, for Dorothy Dawson and Ray McLellan to hold a session on drone search-and-rescue techniques. Drones are used in the backcountry to help teams find lost hikers and to help border patrollers catch undocumented immigrants. Drones can deliver emergency supplies to disaster zones. In fact, in Africa, they're using them to stop elephant poachers, and here in Bella Coola —"

"— they can find bears in distress," I finish for him, making sure he doesn't hurt Min-jun by using the phrase *bear poachers*.

"Yes!" a few listeners respond. As they help themselves to the last dumplings, I put my arm around Dorothy's shoulders and she snuggles up closer. My face is glowing like the campfire.

An hour later, Mom and Dad drop me off at the hospital to visit Granddad. They're on their way to one of their counselling sessions. Sometimes in the clinic I see them brush hands as they bustle about in their stiff white lab coats. Once I caught them kissing. Gross. But they're trying, for sure. And taking more time off to spend with me.

Granddad is lying in his hospital bed, hooked up to way too many tubes and machines. I touch his gaunt cheek.

"Ray," he says weakly, in almost a gurgle, and lifts a paper-thin hand that I take gently in mine. Mr. Kim's arrest "took the stuffing" out of him, he confessed the day after it happened. He has gone downhill since. Or maybe he was going to anyway. The cancer is winning the fight.

"Time to meet me Maker," he says in a tired whisper, green eyes on my face. "Some things you can't stop from coming at you, even with a marshmallow stick and a rock."

I hang my head but allow a hint of a smile.

"How're the young bears doing?"

"Two had to be put down," I report with a thick voice. "Hank and the other one are going to make it. We'll release them into the mountains when they're ready."

"That's good. Good," he says, patting my hand. "Taught them men a good lesson after they went arseways, didn't you? You and yer wee wannabe planes. Even if you jailed half me best clients."

I nod, not knowing what to say.

"Yer a smart boy like yer dad and granddad, I know that. Got the instincts. Anderson says yer a hero, did everything right and put proud to the McLellan name."

Then he launches into a coughing fit, followed by silence.

"Yer mom brought in some o' her Manhattan chowder," he finally says, like it's an important announcement. "An' I thanked her for it."

"Yeah, and how was it?" I ask.

"Better than the gruel they serve here!"

He closes his eyes for a long time, and a shiver of fear runs through me.

"Granddad?" I say, leaning down near his face. "I love you."

His eyes flutter open. Wetness collects in them. His fingers rise to my left ear, and he touches it gently, like a priest offering a benediction. Then he squeezes my hand with a strength I didn't imagine he still had. A strength of true acceptance.

"Whisht!" he says, a smile lighting up his wrinkled face.

AUTHOR'S NOTE

DRONE CHASE SPRANG, above all, from place: the Great Bear Rainforest, "a global treasure that covers 6.4 million hectares (24,711 square miles) on British Columbia's north and central coast — equivalent in size to Ireland" (greatbearrainforest.gov.bc.ca.).

I always wanted to visit it, and what better excuse than needing to research a novel set in it? Of course, to have teens pursue a bear-poaching gang, I needed to read a lot about bear poaching, which is done primarily for selling the bile (a fluid that is made and released by the liver and stored in the gallbladder) on the black market. Unfortunately, some people believe the myth that bear bile cures almost any ailment, which has spawned "bear bile farms," especially in Asian countries. Reading articles about poaching and bear-bile farms was extraordinarily difficult, literally nauseating, but essential to making my novel authentic.

Is there poaching in BC? In 2017, National Geographic reported, "The fight to protect the bears of the Great Bear Rainforest is [not] over. There are still too few wildlife officers to enforce hunting regulations, which means much of the work will continue to fall to the Coastal Guardian Watchmen, a network of First Nations people who monitor, patrol, and enforce indigenous laws in parts of the Great Bear Rainforest that are too remote for federal or provincial officers to reach regularly."

When I visited Bella Coola to research my novel and to hike, explore, watch grizzly bears, and speak at two local schools, I was totally taken by this stunningly beautiful region. It's high on my list to return there, and you can find photographs of my visit on my blog at pam-withers.com/new-forthcoming-novel-drone-chase/.

While in Bella Coola researching this story, I spoke at Bella Coola Elementary School, where a student named Rayland told me his great-grandfather cared for an abandoned cub till it was ready to go back to the wild. I really appreciated Rayland coming forward like that, and imagine my delight when his father, Hank Bill, was willing to spend time filling me in on details of the cub brought home by his grandfather. Hank clearly remembers bottle-feeding and play-wrestling with the cub as a child:

This was thirty to thirty-five years ago, in the 1980s. Growing up, my grandpa lived on Gang

Ranch near Williams Lake, BC. I was raised off the land. My grandpa lived in the old ways, cowboying and buffalo herding. He owned the largest buffalo herd.

One day Grandpa found an abandoned cub and brought it home. He was still nursing, so they made him a baby bottle. I was curious. He was timid at first. He looked a little scared. I took my time getting to know him. I'd give him his bottle when I was allowed. After he was too old for the bottle, Grandpa fed him fish and buffalo and deer meat.

I used to play with him while growing up. Me and the bear played. He was way stronger. Sometimes he pushed me and I went flying. But he never hurt me or attacked me. I'd tap him and run, and he'd chase. I'd wrestle with him. He'd grab me and throw me around. We didn't really cuddle. He liked to go by the fireplace.

The cub stayed in our backyard. He wasn't fenced or tied up or anything. He could come and go as he pleased. I followed if he went on a walk. He'd go to the creek and play and chase bugs, pretty much did whatever bears do. He'd make normal bear sounds: mmmm, rrrr, umhhh. He'd do his growl.

When the cub was old enough and off the bottle, he left every time the other bears went fishing. But he'd come back to Grandpa's every summer. Grandpa raised him till he was big

PAM WITHERS

*enough to return to the mountains. The cub was
two or three when we let him loose.*

Organizations that work against bear poaching
include World Animal Protection (worldanimalpro
tection.org), the Humane Society (hsi.org), Animals
Asia Foundation (animalsasia.org), Justice for BC
Grizzlies (justiceforbcgrizzlies.com), and Pacific Wild
(pacificwild.org).

ACKNOWLEDGEMENTS

MY MAIN CONSULTANT on this book was Rob Brooks, a Vancouver-based sales and marketing professional who owns and operates Altair UAV (altairuav.com). He was more than patient in helping me develop plot scenes, in explaining technical aspects, and in reading my first drafts, even contributing his own writing in places. I also had advice from droner Brian McLellan of Mayne Island, BC.

Steve Hodgson, BC Parks Area Supervisor for Bella Coola Valley, confirmed that Bent Ear, Lady Diver, Y-Bear, and the Rowdy Twins are actual bears in the Great Bear Rainforest.

Mayne Island veterinarian Elisabeth Jahren "vetted" all sections connected with animal care. Married to a fellow vet, with kids who all but grew up in vet clinics, she says she can relate to Ray and his parents.

To ensure that Mr. Kim's dialogue was authentic, I ran portions of the manuscript past Ann Y.K. Choi (annykchoi.com), a Toronto-based author and educator originally from South Korea. She read Mr. Kim's dialogue aloud to her family, which prompted some corrections and discussion, then translated his words into Korean and had a Korean Canadian friend translate them back to English. How overwhelmingly grateful I am for her above-and-beyond feedback!

It was in Doug Peacock's *Grizzly Years: In Search of the American Wilderness* that I read about a bear blowing and popping bubbles in a mud hole.

In *Great Bear Wild: Dispatches from a Northern Rainforest* by Ian McAllister, I came across the phrase "ursine daycare" (cubs waiting in trees for their moms to finish catching salmon or collecting berries).

The line "Skinned, a bear looks eerily human," comes from Kevin Van Tighem in *Bears Without Fear*.

The reference to bear gallbladders being sold in velvet-lined boxes comes from Ben Kavoussi in a March 24, 2011, article at sciencebasedmedicine.org.

Special hugs to Deb Rowe, who accompanied me to Bella Coola.

And finally, thanks to my teen editor, Vansh Bali.

ABOUT THE AUTHOR

AWARD-WINNING AUTHOR Pam Withers has written numerous bestselling outdoor-adventure novels for teens. She is also a popular presenter in schools, libraries, and at writers' and educators' conferences. Pam has worked as a journalist, magazine editor, book editor, and associate publisher. She discovered whitewater kayaking in college and pursued slalom kayak racing for many years, and has also spent time as a whitewater kayak instructor, whitewater raft guide, and teen summer-camp coordinator. Pam continues to enjoy time in the outdoors when not writing or indulging in her latest passion, table tennis. She divides her time between Vancouver and the Gulf Islands, British Columbia.